SPRING'S DELIGHT

COWBOY SEASON BOOK FOUR

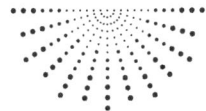

KATHLEEN BALL

This is for you, Dad with all my love!

And to Bruce, Steven, Colt and Clara because I love you.

CHAPTER ONE

Colt O'Malley stood watching the sunrise in the big, Montana spring sky. He hadn't slept, how could he? In fact, he hadn't slept for days. Burying his brother, Caleb hadn't been part of his plan, ever, but plans change in the most drastic ways.

As he rubbed his hand over his unshaven jaw, he was surprised at the length of his stubble. He hadn't changed his clothes in a few days either. As soon as he'd gotten home from the funeral, he'd thrown on some old clothes and rushed to the barn to muck stalls with the hope that keeping busy would distract him from dwelling on the heaviness of his heart. The last few days had been a horribly painful blur. It really didn't matter how he looked. He didn't care anymore. The only thing that still made sense was caring for the horses. They relied on him to get them well and to keep them safe. They were the only reason he got out of bed. They needed him.

Nothing worked not excessive physical exertion and certainly not large amounts of whiskey. He'd tried both routes but neither helped, and bitterness filled his heart. He was a lone cowboy now. Caleb had been the last of his family, now he was gone too. Everyone was gone, and he was the sole owner of the ranch, land handed down over the centuries. The legacy would end with him.

Grabbing his Stetson and coat, he headed outside. The ranch was cold, bitter even, and it matched his mood. There was plenty of snow, but he'd already plowed and shoveled yesterday so he'd have to find something else to tire him out today. Maybe if he moved some of the massive, round hay bales, he would finally exhaust himself and be able to pass out. Yeah right, he'd probably never sleep again.

He noticed a truck coming up his long drive and swore. Why couldn't people just leave him alone? It had been a week, and everyone still felt the need to try to cheer him up. Well, he'd had about all he could take. He didn't want any more condolences or flowers, and he certainly didn't want another casserole delivered; the women of Carlston weren't very good cooks. The urge to go back in the house and slam the door was powerful, but he stood waiting for the truck to come closer. He'd just send the busybody on their way.

His brow furrowed. Old Ed, the town loner, had a passenger with him. Old Ed didn't like anyone bothering him so Colt thought, out of everyone, Old Ed would know to leave him alone. No one knew anything about Ed except that he moved to Carlston about forty years ago. A nice enough guy but he never talked much and he didn't answer questions.

Colt didn't miss the shrug Ed gave him as he walked over to the passenger-side door. Colt widened his stance and crossed his arms. Whoever was with him was going right back to town.

"This young miss was supposed to meet Caleb at the bus station. Didn't know what to tell the gal so I brought her out to you."

"Just take her back. Caleb never mentioned a girlfriend," Colt snapped.

The girl walked toward him, her blue eyes were wide and filled with confusion. Hell, she didn't know, and he'd have to be the one to tell her. *Damn, why didn't Ed tell her?*

"Caleb told me to come." Her chin wobbled a bit, but she stared him straight in the eye. There was strength and determination in her eyes but it was tempered by her obvious nervousness. She didn't seem like Caleb's type, fun loving and clueless. Something was off about her.

Colt shook his head. The girl wore a light jacket and sneakers, and she didn't even have a hat to cover her lush, red hair. No, she didn't belong here, and Caleb would have mentioned a new girl in his life.

"Caleb is dead. We laid him to rest three days ago. You'll just have to go back to where you came from." He made his voice as gruff as possible hoping she would turn and run.

She took a step back and covered her mouth with her cold-reddened hand. "I saw him in Texas just before the school break. He can't be dead. We…we had plans. Are you sure?"

"I'm damn sure. He's dead and buried. Just go home. There's nothing for you here. Go back to Texas and live your life. Finish college." He gestured to Ed. "Take her back, and put her on a bus home."

HER WHOLE WORLD SLOWED, and she stared at this man with an aching chest. Her best friend was dead? How could he be dead? Caleb was the most vividly alive person she knew. He constantly delighted her with stories of his brother and ranch life. Turning away she only saw snow and more snow. Piles of it were everywhere. Her body chilled, and she shook her head. It couldn't be true. Caleb would walk right out of the house, give her a big, bear hug and laugh. However, the pain in his brother's eyes crushed her; she wasn't going to see Caleb ever again. Now what? There was no going back. She bit the inside of her cheek as she turned back toward Colt.

His brown eyes were filled with grief. The heavy shadows under his eyes indicated a lack of sleep, and his shoulders slumped in defeat as though he was about to fall over.

Wrapping her arms around her middle, she stared at him. He was a big man, tall with wide shoulders. Somehow, he looked shrunken. "I'll stay and make sure you eat. I'm assuming the job is still open."

Colt took off his tan Stetson and slapped it against his thigh. His dark hair hung past his collar, and it looked soft blowing in the cold wind. "Look, I don't know what the hell you are talking about. There is no job. I don't know what Caleb told you, if he really invited you here at all. It's not his style to bring girls home."

Spring's heart was in a vice that kept tightening. "He offered me a job keeping the books for you."

"Ed, take her back." The bitterness in his tone was loud and clear.

"No can do. This little gal was promised a job, and I think you should honor that promise."

"Then leave, I'll take her back myself."

"Fine." Old Ed turned and walked to his truck. When he got the door, he turned toward Colt. "You know I don't go around handing out advice, but if I was judging by the way you look, I'd say she needs to stay."

Colt's eyes raked her over, making her nervous. Finally, he sighed. "Let's go inside, and get you something warm to wear before I take you back."

Numb inside and out, she followed him. The house looked

much bigger than she'd pictured. The exterior was wood, covered in peeling paint, but the front porch looked ample. It was hard to judge, however, with all the blowing snow.

Walking inside, she shivered. It was spring break, and she thought it might be chilly still, but she didn't have the money to buy a heavier coat or boots. She felt stupid arriving in her windbreaker and sneakers. The snow must be due to melt soon. Warmth was in full bloom in Texas already. Sure, there was a bit of snow remaining at home, but this whole area was still a blanket of cold, white snow.

The front part of the house had an open floor plan, the kitchen and great room were connected, and a roaring fire in the massive stone fireplace welcomed her.

"Have a seat, I'll make coffee."

Spring nodded and cleared a place on the cluttered, threadbare couch. Caleb hadn't exaggerated when he'd told her that they were barely keeping their heads above water. She didn't mind poor. It was what she'd known all her life.

Caleb had held out a helping hand when he invited her to work at the ranch. He knew what she'd been through, but it didn't look as though she'd be staying.

"So what did Caleb promise you? Were you two going to share a room?" Colt leaned his long body against the kitchen counter staring at her.

Swallowing hard, her eyes widened as she stared back. She'd done nothing to deserve this. "Caleb was the best friend I ever had. I was in a bad situation, and he offered to help."

"How were you planning to pay him back? You were planning to pay him back, weren't you?"

"It wasn't…we weren't…we were just friends. He used to come to the diner I worked at every evening to study and drink coffee. I believed his offer of a job was genuine. Caleb didn't seem the type that would have wanted me to pay him back."

Colt sighed and nodded. He grabbed two mugs from the wooden cupboard, and poured the coffee. "Anything in it?"

"No, black is fine."

Colt stood before her looking even bigger. He handed her a mug and sat in a chair to the left of the couch. "You knew Caleb."

Spring was surprised that it was a statement instead of a question. "Yes. He was my best friend. I understand why you don't want me here but truthfully, I have twenty-seven dollars to my name. He said that the pay would be sparse, but there'd be a roof over my head, and a place I could feel safe. I quit my job."

COLT KNEW he was a goner as soon as he looked into her shimmering eyes. To know Caleb was to know his generosity in all things. "Hell, I don't even know your name."

"It's Spring Reed." She took her flimsy coat off exposing a too thin, angular figure.

"Tell me what the job entailed."

Giving him a skeptical look, she proceeded to explain. "He planned to teach me how to do the paperwork. He said that you hated paperwork the most, and he wasn't organized enough to do a good job at it. He also asked if I'd help with the cooking occasionally. He mentioned you were a good cook as long as it came out of a can."

That much was true. They did eat canned meals, and he did hate paperwork. The ache in his heart grew knowing Caleb had been looking to help him. He shrugged. "I haven't even had time to keep up with the bookkeeping. I guess the best I can do is give it a try. Caleb trusted you enough to invite you here. That's good enough for me. Caleb was good at sizing up a person's character. He had a knack for picking out whose word was good and whose wasn't."

Spring nodded and appeared relieved. She sipped her coffee, lost in thought for a moment. She put the cup down and gazed at him. "What happened to Caleb? How did he die?"

More pain and regret washed over him. He didn't want to tell the story again, but she deserved to know. "It was a snowmobile accident. It happened a week ago. The snow was coming down hard and fast, and little Rachael from next door called over here crying because her dog Snoopy was lost in the snow. You must know how Caleb was always trying to fix everything."

Colt noticed she winced at his last words. She was probably someone Caleb was trying to fix. Her story had a ring of truth to it, and on his brother's behalf, he felt honor bound to give her a chance.

"Caleb charged out into the snow, determined to help Rachael."

"Did he find Snoopy?"

He ran his hand over his face. "Yes, he did."

"That's good."

The silence in the room grew as the minutes ticked by, and he wondered if he should be talking. What was there to say?

She was a little bit of a thing, and he thought there was something wrong with her shoulder since she flinched when she moved it. The house was in a shambles. Between being busy with the horses and Caleb's death, he hadn't picked up at all. Glancing around, the amount of clutter astounded him.

"I'm not an easy man to get along with lately. I don't want to be cheered up, and I don't want you to tell me how or when to grieve. In fact, the less we talk the better." Standing up, he gazed at her. She stiffened. "I'm going to find you a sweater. Think about what I said before you take the job."

Standing, he walked to Caleb's room, opened the door and closed it behind him. He leaned against it, closing his eyes, trying to block out the image of Caleb's broken body. The hole in his heart grew daily, and he didn't know how to make it stop. Pushing away from the door, he found a sweater in the back of Caleb's closet. He honestly couldn't remember Caleb ever wearing it. Spring might as well get some use out of it. Lord knew Caleb didn't need it anymore.

She was another waif of Caleb's. It wasn't unusual in the least. Only instead of an injured animal, he'd brought a troubled woman to the ranch.

SPRING DRANK the last of her coffee, grateful it warmed her insides. There wasn't even an open spot for her to place it on the coffee table. She was needed here, and it wouldn't be charity; she'd be working for her keep. A hard man, so different from Caleb's description, she hoped she could get along with him.

Colt returned with a navy blue cardigan. He walked toward her and handed it to her. She put it on, wincing as she stretched her arm into the sleeves. "What's wrong with your shoulder?"

Ashamed, she looked away. "It's nothing. Thanks for the sweater."

He didn't say a word, and the silence grew uncomfortable. Glancing back, she was surprised to find him staring at her.

Colt reached down, took her arm, pushed up her sleeve and swore. "Those are some pretty nasty bruises. Is that what Caleb was helping you with?"

Pulling her arm away, she pushed her sleeve back down. "Yes." It came out as barely a whisper.

"Your shoulder?"

"The same. It hardly bothers me."

"Caleb was right to invite you here. Like I said, I'm not easy to get along with these days, but I do treat women with respect. Right now I have to tend to the animals, but I'll make us something to eat when I get back."

"I'd be happy to make something. I mean I don't want to just sit around waiting until you have time to teach me the job."

"You can help out as soon as those bruises are gone."

Watching him leave, relief rushed through her. It was so hard to read him. He wasn't the easy going brother Caleb told her about. He might not be agreeable or likeable even, but she had a place to stay for now. She hoped by moving to Montana, her ex-boyfriend, Billy would leave her alone and move on.

The urge to be useful filled her, and she walked to the sink. She began cleaning the great, big pile of dishes. As soon as she had the sink cleared, she filled it again with the over-flow of dishes strewn all over the counter. With some elbow grease, she just might have enough room to cook. Her shoulder hurt, but she'd endured far worse. For now, she'd mourn her friend and do a good job.

It seemed incredibly odd to be at the ranch without Caleb. Her heart ached remembering his many kindnesses and contagious laugh. She'd had one true friend, and now she had none.

Why didn't doing the dishes take more thought? Memories of Caleb made her heart and her head, ache. Caleb's passing was shocking and not knowing if she would have, a place to stay long-term scared her.

"I told you I'd take care of breakfast."

The masculine voice startled her, and Spring whirled around, her soapy hands losing their grip on a glass that dropped to the floor and shattered. Colt took a step toward her, and she immediately readied for a fight. Her stance grew wider and her body tensed, but Colt didn't come any closer. *Why can't I be normal?*

"It's all right. I'll just grab the broom." Colt didn't look angry.

"I'm not usually so clumsy. Really, I'm not."

"Hey, it's no big deal. It's only a glass." He vaguely smiled at her and began to sweep it up.

It was as though she was cemented where she stood, and she didn't know how to react. A broken glass was more than enough reason for Billy to hit her. Caleb was a gentle soul and from all the stories of ranch life he told, she assumed Colt was too. While her first impression hadn't been the best, perhaps Colt did have a kind heart buried beneath his grief.

She still refused to let her guard down for a stranger, even Caleb's brother. Colt had a gruff aloofness to him. "I'll replace it."

He straightened up, dumped the glass in the dustpan into the trash and shook his head. "Like I said, it's just a glass."

After she looked into his eyes and still didn't see any anger, she relaxed a bit. "I'll have breakfast cooked in a jiffy."

"Tell you what, you wash and I'll dry. It'll go much faster with two." He grabbed a towel.

Spring nodded and with more care washed the rest of the dishes. She couldn't keep her thoughts off Colt. She couldn't tell what he was thinking, and it made her nervous, she was all too familiar with this feeling. Swallowing hard, she continued to focus on washing until all the dishes shined.

"The kitchen looks nice. It's bigger than I first thought. "

"I bet once I get the rest of the house straightened, it'll

seem big too. It's been lonely here while Caleb was away at college." His voice grew husky.

She surprised herself by touching his arm. "I know all about lonely. I'm grateful that you're giving me this chance."

He looked down at her hand, then at her face. What he looked for, she had no idea. "If Caleb thought enough of you to have you come all the way out here, then the least I can do is get to know you."

After breakfast, Colt left. A man of few words it seemed. He'd helped make bacon and eggs, ate and then took off without even saying when he'd be back. He did point across the great room, to one of the closed doors indicating that room was to be hers.

Grabbing her beat-up suitcase, Spring opened the door to her new room. It was dusty and needed airing out but otherwise it looked nice. An old, faded blue and green quilt, patterned to look like stars, covered a full-size bed. She reached out and touched the softness, tracing the pattern of stitches with her finger. A thing like that had history and part of her yearned to know it.

Next to the bed was a night table with a bible, a book of poems and a glass lamp with a faded shade. The only other piece of furniture was a tall dresser that had seen better days.

The scarred, wood floor was bound to be cold, especially in the mornings. She didn't own slippers so she'd have to keep a pair of socks on the nightstand. Overall, it was paradise.

Everything would be fine if she could find a common ground with Colt. It was bound to be awkward living with someone you didn't know, and his cold exterior was not at all inviting. There was a kindness in him though.

After setting her few belongings in the room, she wandered back to the kitchen and checked the fridge. Truthfully, there wasn't much to check other than some ketchup, bread, cheese and three mason jars of homemade pickles. She decided on grilled cheese sandwiches with some canned tomato soup. Unfortunately, she ended up eating alone since Colt didn't show up for lunch.

At loose ends, she decided to tackle the great room. Being idle didn't sit well with her. Besides, she didn't relish having to go back out into the cold, suitcase in hand. She worked hard until everything gleamed and smelled like lemons. Things she couldn't find a place for she piled in a chair. It looked to be all Colt's stuff, but she didn't dare open his bedroom door without permission.

The house was cozy and simple. The kitchen dominated the right side with the great room between it and the bedrooms. The bathroom was the last door toward the back of the house while her room was the first. One of those doors was Caleb's room, she knew, but she refused to dwell on it.

The floors needed cleaning, but by this time, the adrenaline was trickling away and exhaustion hit her hard. A big bay window graced the front of the kitchen, and she walked over to stand before it, gazing at the snow. Being from Texas, she'd never seen so much snow in her life. It sparkled in the sun like diamonds, engulfing the outbuildings in its splendor. Gazing across the wide drive, she saw the barn. It, like the house, looked sturdy but in need of some TLC.

Her pay had never been discussed, but if she could make enough for warm clothes, that would be fine. If she stayed long, she could definitely use them.

Two other trucks were parked in the driveway. They probably belonged to the people who work for Colt. He'd have to have help to work a ranch wouldn't he? Caleb often talked about cattle and horses. She might have lived in Texas, but she'd never been on a horse, and she couldn't wait to see one. Looking down at her worn sneakers, she knew it wouldn't be soon.

There was something beside the barn, and after a moment of trying to discern what it was, her hand covered her mouth and she gasped. A mangled snowmobile sat there. How could Colt stand to have it on the property? Looking at it made her shiver, and tears trailed down her face. Caleb was really gone and her heart broke for his brother.

Spotting Colt walking toward the house, she dashed away her tears with the heels of her hands and scurried away from the window. She didn't want him to think she was spying on him.

COLT STAMPED his feet on the porch, trying to remove as much packed on snow from his boots as possible. He opened the door and quickly shut it behind him. It didn't take more than a couple seconds to make the house cold.

The smell of lemon hit him in a wave. He glanced up as he removed his boots and sought Spring out. He frowned when he saw her reddened eyes. "What's wrong?"

"Memories I guess, but I'm fine. You must be hungry." She hustled to the stove and turned it on.

"I could eat. I forgot about lunch, but I haven't had much of an appetite lately." He took off his tan Stetson and hung it on the peg near the door. "Was there even anything to make?"

"Grilled cheese and soup. Your cupboards are pretty bare."

"Them church ladies tried to give me casseroles and such, but I refused most of them." The surprise in her eyes caused his face to warm. "They just wanted to get into my business. Busybodies, every one of them. Besides there is only one woman who knows how to cook in this town, her name is Autumn. The rest, well, I couldn't manage to choke their food down."

"Oh."

"I didn't go to the store for the same reason. They just want to fuss over me, and it only makes things worse."

Spring placed soup and a sandwich in front of him. "I can understand that."

"Really?" He cocked his right eyebrow. "No one else seems to."

She gave him a whisper of a smile. "I know about being in pain, and wanting to be left alone."

Colt had to look away. She was too sincere, and he wasn't sure he wanted understanding. She might know pain, but his suffering was his own. For a moment, he wondered what her story was, but he finished eating in silence then pushed back from the table. "I'll be back at sundown. Make what you can. I'll have Bibbs bring supplies tomorrow."

He put on his boots, coat and Stetson. Turning, he gazed at her. The corners of her mouth drooped, and his heart went out to her. Quickly, before he said something foolish, he went out into the snow.

Brr, it's cold. A burst of frigid air blew snow into his eyes. There was nothing worse than a springtime snowstorm. Right when you were making plans for the future...

He didn't have a plan anymore. He always thought he'd work side by side with Caleb, growing the ranch but his future died and was buried. He felt gut sick, and he swore his head was going to explode. A feeling of being lost engulfed him. Sighing, he shook his head. Maybe having her around wouldn't be so bad. He'd been losing too much weight, and he'd have to change his clothes more often.

At least he had his horses. The horses needed him. A lot of the time, they took his mind off his misery at least for a short while. He loved what he did, but he wished there was no need for a horse rescue. He never understood why people got horses then neglected them. Caleb thought that people didn't realize the time and commitment a horse needed and chose to give up. Whatever the reason, it was a big problem, and thank God, Holden O'Leary and Jonas Barnes had his back, especially now. Stone McCoy used to, and he never would have guessed what a hardhearted man he really was.

Not one tiny word from his supposed friend about Caleb's death. Perhaps he needed to change his way of looking at the world. In the past, he always gave people the benefit of the doubt until they proved otherwise and unfortunately, Stone showed his true colors. From now on, he should make people earn his trust first. Sighing, he walked on into the barn, gazing at all the horses who stuck their heads out of their stalls to greet him. His brain wasn't wired that way, and suspicion didn't come naturally to him.

SPRING STIRRED the big stainless steel pot. She'd thrown together some chili and she had cornbread all ready to go into the oven. It was hard to judge if the chili was spicy enough for Colt without knowing much about him. Putting it on low, she put the lid on the pot.

What she wanted most right now was a hot shower. She felt so grubby from her travels, and since Colt wouldn't be back until sundown, she had a chance for privacy.

She carried her toiletries into the bathroom, undressed and turned the shower on. Right before she stepped in she remembered she'd left her razor in the bedroom. Wrapping a green towel around her, she scurried to her room to grab it. Hurrying back to the shower, she tripped on an uneven part of the floor.

Letting go of the towel, she braced herself for the impact with her arms. Her towel went one way and her razor another. On her hands and knees, she could now see close-up that the floor did indeed need scrubbing. She reached over and grabbed the razor as she stood again, taking a step toward the towel.

The sound of the door opening made her freeze. Colt walked through the door and she screamed. As quickly as she could, she snatched the towel from the floor, ran into the bathroom and slammed the door. Her heart beat frantically as she leaned against it. *Oh my*. Spring felt herself blush from head to toe.

Looking in the mirror she shrugged, there wasn't much worth seeing anyway and certainly nothing to blush about, or so she tried to tell herself. She was a thin mass of bruises.

With trembling hands, she washed and dried herself. She'd wanted to make a good impression, but it would be impossible now. Why it even mattered so much, she wasn't certain. She put on a pair of old jeans and a yellow T-shirt, allowing her long red hair to fall down her back to air-dry.

Bravery was required to open the door, so she stared at the door handle for a minute or two to steel herself before finally turning it. Holding her breath, she opened it. She let that breath out again when there was no sign of Colt on the other side.

Her heart began to slow, but she was a bit jittery. How she wished Caleb were here to pave the way. Caleb knew all about her past and he'd been the one warm, bright spot in her dark, cold world. Colt probably wouldn't even ask unless Billy somehow found her. Actually, she hoped he didn't ask because she didn't want to talk about it.

Stirring the chili, she heard the door open and close. Too embarrassed to turn around, she simply kept stirring. No footsteps, he must be waiting at the door. Finally, she turned putting her hands on her burning cheeks. "I'm sorry you had to see that."

Colt's brow furrowed. "It's me who's sorry. Truthfully, it was just an accident, and I didn't look."

The glint in his eyes and the suppressed smile gave the impression he did see everything, but she nodded at him and pulled the cornbread out of the oven. "Dinner is just about ready."

"It's a real treat to have dinner all made for me. I almost always do the cooking except for when Caleb…"

The stark look on his face made her want to hug him. "He was your brother. You're bound to talk about him now and again. I feel the depth of your loss, and I wish I knew how to help you, but I don't."

Colt nodded and took off his boots, jacket and his hat. He ran his hand through his brown hair. "I reckon I can see why Caleb was so taken with you."

"Oh, it was never like that. He was a friend who wanted to help. But that's beside the point. Dinner is ready. I made chili, and I hope I made it hot enough."

"Honey, there has never been a bowl of chili I couldn't handle."

"Good, I was a little nervous."

They both sat down, and Colt smiled at her. "Looks good." He took a big spoonful of chili, and he seemed to enjoy it. Then his eyes suddenly began to water, and his face turned beet red.

"Are you choking?"

He shook his head and croaked out. "Hot."

Spring took a bite and smiled. "This is mild in Texas. I was shooting for hotter, but I missed."

He ran to the sink and quickly turned on the faucet, filling a big glass with water. As he gulped it down, his crimson face started to turn back to normal. "This is mild in

Texas? Good Lord, honey, what are their stomachs made of?"

"Steel of course." She smiled. He had gotten annoyed, and he didn't try to take it out on her. Colt's outsides were steel, but he really wasn't so hard on the inside.

CHAPTER TWO

$\mathcal{C}$olt left the house as soon as he finished eating. He couldn't believe that one little gal could affect him so much so soon. She pulled on his heart and that he couldn't allow. Pity, but that's the way it had to be. Obviously, she'd been hurt, and Caleb's death must have come as a real blow to her. It had been a blow to everyone. No, he wasn't going to get close to anyone again; it hurt too damn much when they were gone.

After making sure the horses were all fed and watered, he stood in front of Heavy Duty's stall and waited for the quarter horse to check his shirt pocket. It was a nightly ritual. The only difference was this time his mind wasn't on the ranch or Caleb.

It felt good and right to offer her a place to stay and a job. A slight smile crossed his face as he thought about that afternoon. He couldn't remember the last time he'd glimpsed a naked woman, and now he wished he'd looked.

Already she was changing his thinking, he could tell. Maybe his dad was right, maybe women were bad news. Colt had heard his father say it often enough. It wasn't that his mother had left; she died and left behind two scared boys and a bitter husband.

Dating came naturally. All he had to do was smile. He was known as quite the flirt around town, but then there was the damn emotional stuff. Whatever happened to no strings attached? Every woman he'd shown any interest in, automatically thought of marriage. He always figured that Caleb would be the one to have a family, with sons to pass the ranch down to. A silenced dream that would never come true.

Damn it. Colt pulled his jacket collar up around his face. He longed to be inside by his fireplace. If it'd been warmer, he'd just wait until he was certain she was asleep, but in this bitter cold, he didn't have that luxury. He gave Heavy Duty a grim look and made the cold march to the house.

Colt walked in and immediately his gaze was drawn to the couch where Spring lay, a green blanket covering her. Light from the fire bathed her, making her look achingly beautiful.

Quietly, he walked to the couch and looked at her. She had circles under her eyes. Poor girl was worn down to the nub. Traveling all that way, and then jumping straight into overhauling his house, it was no wonder. Colt placed his hands under her and lifted her into his arms. Even though he knew she was thin, she was much lighter than he'd imagined. Her eyelashes swept across her face, at the top of her high cheekbones. They were a light color, much lighter than her bright hair. The sprinkling of freckles across her cheeks gave her a childlike appearance.

She didn't move until he started to place her on the bed. Her eyes opened, and all hell broke loose. She screamed and fought him, kicking and scratching. Spring was more like a feral cat than a sweet gal.

Instantly, Colt let her go and stepped back. Touching his cheek, he found that he was bleeding.

Wide-eyed, Spring stared at him. "Oh no, Colt, I'm sorry! I didn't know it was you. I didn't remember where I was." She got up from the bed and closed the distance between them. Her hand touched his cheek where it bled, and doubt appeared in her eyes.

Colt felt her pulling on his heart again. What was it with this girl? "I'm fine. I'm sorry I scared you." He backed away toward the door. "Goodnight." He hurried out of her room.

Colt rubbed the back of his neck as he made his way to his own room. Glimpsing in the mirror, his scratch didn't appear deep. Shaking his head, he sighed. She was going to be trouble.

———

THE NEXT MORNING, Spring jumped out of bed and was certain she set all kinds of records getting dressed so fast. Reading westerns was a favorite pastime for her, and she knew cowboys liked to be up before dawn.

Darkness still enveloped the outdoors as she made coffee. Remembering last night made her heart pound. What if he decided to send her packing? She put two extra scoops of coffee into the coffee maker just in case. Cowboys liked their coffee extra strong didn't they?

She frowned, realizing she really didn't know anything real about cowboys or ranching. At the rate she was going, she might not need to know.

When the coffee was ready, she sat at the big oak table and ran her hands over all of the dents and scratches. There was even a tiny letter C carved into it. She wondered if it was Colt or Caleb who had put it there. She reached for her coffee and took a sip, almost spitting it out on the floor. It tasted strong and bitter, and she hoped that Colt liked it that way.

It surprised her that Colt hadn't gotten up yet. It wasn't quite sunrise, but didn't he need to milk the cow and feed the horses? She stood up and walked to the window. Her brow furrowed. There was no one in sight.

She grabbed the sweater Colt had given her and headed outside to the porch to watch the sunrise. Finally, the sun rose in hues of orange, purple and yellow with a dusting of pink. It was a remarkable sight.

The door behind her opened, and her body automatically jerked. Glancing over her shoulder, she saw Colt's perplexed expression.

"Get inside. Damn it's cold! What are you doing out here?"

"Watching the sunrise." Without looking at him, she scooted past his hard body and went inside.

Shutting the door behind him, he leaned his tall frame against it. "Why are you up so early? Couldn't you sleep after last night?" Concern crossed his face.

"I wanted to have your coffee ready for when you got up to milk the cow."

Colt's lips twitched, and he glanced away. His laughter started as a rumble deep in his chest that bubbled over. He turned toward her and bit his lip, but he started laughing again.

Wrapping her arms around herself, her pride stung. Why shouldn't he laugh at her, everyone else seem to, except for Caleb.

"I'm sorry, honey." He grabbed the coffee pot and poured himself a cup. He tried to look somber, but it wasn't working. Taking a sip of the coffee, he spit it out and started laughing again.

Spring flew to her room and slammed the door. She

didn't fit in here and she didn't fit with Colt. She'd grown up with enough people laughing at her. She'd been told time, after time she was useless and hopeless and she was tired of it. Her foundation was made of sand, constantly shifting and blowing away but she always tried to stand strong. Sitting on the bed, she traced the star pattern on the quilt with her finger. Somehow, she thought she'd find firm footing here, a firm foundation to stand on, but now she wasn't so sure.

There was a light knock followed by the door opening. Colt leaned against the doorframe, his wide shoulders filled the whole doorway.

"I didn't mean to upset you, and I shouldn't have laughed." He looked somewhat contrite. At least he wasn't laughing anymore.

"I'm fine. It takes more than a little laughter to upset me," she bluffed.

"I'm sorry all the same. It's not my way to hurt others. I know I'm gruff, and hell that was the first time I've laughed in months. I've never seen anyone scramble so quickly. I usually get up at sunrise, have a quick bite to eat, and head out. Some days I bring lunch with me, and other days I stop home for lunch. Dinner is after sunset."

Spring nodded.

"Oh, one more thing, I'm not like those cowboys you read about or see in movies. I don't like my coffee so strong that it'll take the polish off my belt buckle." He smiled. "It'll be fine, really, we need to adjust to each other but we'll be fine."

COLT STARED at the horribly mangled snowmobile. It was a twisted piece of metal and fiberglass. No one could have survived such destruction. If only he had gone looking for the damn dog instead of Caleb. Hell, he wouldn't have gone looking, not in that storm. It'd been the worst storm of the season. What was Rachael doing out in the storm with Snoopy anyway? The temptation to go over to the McCoy's house and kick her father's ass grew stronger every day.

Why hadn't Stone McCoy gone out looking for that good-for-nothing dog? Colt kicked the snowmobile then winced at the throbbing in his foot. He thought about getting it hauled away, but he just couldn't. Caleb bought the blasted thing himself, and he was so proud of all the hard work he'd done to earn the money for it. The ache in his heart over-whelmed him, and he was on an emotional overload.

Caleb was always a sucker for a damsel in distress. Colt had always admired Caleb's kindness but now... "Damn it, Caleb, why did you have to go, and look for that mangy animal?" His words drifted away on the snowflakes. No one would hear them. No one would answer them. No one cared.

He was doing just fine before Spring arrived. He'd hard-ened his heart and let his bitterness take control, and it worked just fine for him. Dang blasted female! She was making him feel all over again, but Caleb meant to help her so he'd honor Caleb's plan as hard as it may be.

He'd have to use the other snowmobile to take the hay to the cattle. They were probably scattered in this weather. Spring in Montana was harsh and unpredictable, but up until the last week, he'd thought he'd had a good life. Now he wasn't so sure. Maybe all the hard work wasn't worth it. What did he really have to show for it? He wouldn't get anything out of it if he sold and with the economy the way it was, his ranch wasn't worth much. The land was worth plenty, but the thought of it sectioned into housing units made him gut sick. Ranching was in his blood and it always would be.

Glancing at the house, he found his bitterness abating. Milking the cow at dawn and mud coffee? He shook his head and his lips twitched. She tried hard, but she clearly wasn't a country girl. It would take a bit to get used to having a female in the house but for Caleb's sake, he'd give it his best shot. Her blue eyes looked too big for her face, and she was as skinny as all get out. He liked her red hair, but she looked as though she hadn't been eating right or something. She needed looking after.

He loaded the snowmobile trailer with hay, got on and started it, looking once again at the house. It made him leery, but for some reason he wanted to be the one to look after her. He told himself it was because he missed Caleb, but deep down he knew it was more. Something about Spring attracted him, and he'd have to be on his guard to be sure it didn't lead anywhere.

SPRING CONTEMPLATED SCRUBBING the wood floor. It really needed cleaning but her shoulder still hurt. Walking over to the mantel, she examined each photo. Her heart hurt for Caleb. It also hurt for Colt. Caleb had told her they had lost their father when Colt was twenty-one and Caleb was sixteen. Caleb never said how he died. He just told her how long and hard Colt worked to keep the ranch going to keep them together.

The door opened, and two burly men entered the house. Spring jumped, and dropped the picture she held as she felt all the blood drain from her face.

"Howdy, ma'am. I didn't mean to scare you witless." The bigger of the two approached her. "I just have a load of food to bring in. This here is Shady and I'm Bibbs."

Spring nodded at them both. The width of Bibbs' shoulders scared her. He was not a man to tangle with, although his kind brown eyes nicely countered his scruffy unshaven look.

Shady on the other hand looked like a young kid. He had blond hair, blue eyes and a great smile. He made her feel more comfortable about having two strange men in the house.

"I remember now. Colt said you'd be by."

"Good thing. There's a storm brewing, and we won't be going back to town anytime soon." Bibbs took the toothpick out of his mouth while he talked and put it back in.

"Looks like you'll have two extra guests around here." Shady went to the door. "I'll start bringing in the supplies."

"You don't live on the ranch? Isn't there a bunk house?"

"Yes but Shady and me bunk in an apartment near town. Shady, he's got himself a lady. Me, I'm free as a bird."

Spring wasn't quite sure what the free as a bird thing was about but he was one bird she'd rather not catch. She just gave a forced smile and went back to her work. Picking up the dropped photo, she was relieved to see the glass hadn't shattered. The photo showed a young Colt holding his baby brother.

"Well, ma'am, that's all of it." Shady smiled at her.

Bibbs slapped him on the back. "We have work to do. See ya."

Watching the door close, she wondered how much they ate. Shady looked thin but sometimes it was the thin guys who could really pack it away. She walked over and examined the supplies they brought in. There was everything from toilet paper to laundry detergent, and there was even a cake along with donuts of all kinds.

She reached for the cake and held it in front of her. She'd seen many cakes, but was the recipient of none. They had no way of knowing it was her birthday in a few days. Usually birthdays and holidays brought nothing but dread and heartache. Growing up in foster homes, she received few gifts here and there. Mostly she watched the real children open their presents. Nonetheless, she wished for the same thing every year. She wanted a loving home. For a brief second she thought she'd get that wish with Billy, but she was wrong, painfully wrong.

When Caleb had invited her to the ranch, anticipation filled her. She knew she'd be there in time for her birthday and hoped to celebrate, but it wouldn't be right to celebrate this year. Perhaps it was just as well.

Bags filled with groceries covered the whole kitchen table. She knew she'd best get them all put away and figure out menus. She didn't know if they would be back for lunch or not, but she planned to be ready.

Lunchtime arrived, and three frozen bodies descended on the fireplace. Spring filled three mugs with coffee and handed them around, glad she'd thought to make it. She watched Colt take a sip. This time she made it right, she hoped.

The bright twinkle in his eyes as he peered over the rim of the mug warmed her. *Whew, he liked it.* "I'll get lunch ready."

"Thank you, ma'am." Bibbs smiled and hung his coat up on one of the pegs near the front door.

Spring smiled at him. "No problem."

She reheated the homemade potato soup she had made earlier and set to making chicken salad sandwiches. She'd also made pumpkin bread. She hoped that she had it right.

She put the last plate on the table. *There, looks good and hopefully the men will like it.* She hadn't realized that she was so nervous until they took their first bite, and each smiled.

"Better than my ma." Shady helped himself to another sandwich.

"Sure is good." Bibbs nodded.

Gazing at Colt, she wondered what he thought. The relaxed smile on his face was all she needed.

They finished it all in record time. She'd never seen people eat so fast. Both Bibbs and Shady thanked her, and then walked toward the door for their coats and hats. Colt hung back.

"You'll do." His smile went right through her and landed in her heart.

"Thanks, take care out there."

He nodded and shrugged into his coat. They left leaving an arctic blast of cold behind.

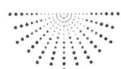

*T*hree days later, a loud pounding at the front door startled Spring. Her hands were sticky with biscuit dough. Grabbing a towel, she ran and opened the door. There stood an incredibly handsome cowboy. His gray eyes were somber as he held a pie in one hand and a doll in the other.

"I just got back from a business trip, and I heard what happened to Caleb. Is Colt around?"

"He's out on the range."

"I'm sorry, where are my manners? I'm Stone McCoy. You see Rachael is my daughter, and I just found out what happened. My wife, Winter, can't seem to stop crying, and Rachael is beside herself. Seems that Snoopy, our dog, got out during the last storm. Winter refused to risk anyone on the ranch by having them go looking for the dog." He shifted from one foot to another. "You must think horribly of me. Are you a relative?"

"Come in before you freeze. I'm Spring, I was a friend of Caleb's. He offered me a job when he left for spring break, and I didn't know what happened until I got here."

Stone closed his eyes and an expression of intense pain crossed his face. "I'm so sorry. I've been friends with the O'Malleys for quite a few years now. I really just wanted to talk to Colt. Winter made him a pie, and Rachael sent him her doll. Her name is Faith."

Spring took his offerings and set them on the bench near the door. She reached out and touched Stone's arm. "It was an accident. You can come in and wait, or if you'd rather I'll tell Colt you were here."

Stone looked down at her hand, and he appeared lost in thought for a moment. Nodding his head, he opened the door then turned his haunted, gray eyes on her and stared. Finally, he nodded again and left.

Spring wanted to go into her room and hide as her grief rushed back anew. Nothing would bring Caleb back, and nothing would bring Colt's happiness back. Instead, she walked back to the kitchen counter, placing both the pie and the doll on it. Unfortunately, she'd learned the hard way there was no way to hide.

SHADY LAUGHED THEN ADMONISHED Bibbs for not doing his fair share of the day's work. "How'd you know that pecan pie is my favorite?" Bibbs smiled and winked at her.

"Actually it came from Mr. McCoy."

Shady and Bibbs exchanged glances. Shady shrugged then gave Spring a smile "Did he mention if the roads were passable?"

Biting her bottom lip, she shook her head. "I don't even know how he got here. I didn't think to ask."

"He got here by horse; the tracks are outside in the snow." Bibbs smiled. "It's coming down hard out there. Guess we get to spend the night with you after all."

"I'd best get out there and shovel off the porch." Shady tipped his hat to her.

Spring went back to chopping carrots for her beef stew. She learned a thing or two about cooking, working at the diner.

Bibbs walked right up behind her, so close that she could feel the heat of him. Spring closed her eyes, trying her best to remain calm. She did have a knife in her hand.

"Mmm, smells so good."

Spring didn't turn around. "Would you mind stepping back a bit? It makes me nervous."

Bibbs took a big step back. "Sorry, ma'am."

Spring turned, his brown eyes were full of concern "I've had a hard time of it lately, and it kind of freaks me out to have a man too close."

"Don't you worry, ma'am. I know what it's like. I didn't mean no disrespect."

"I know that, Bibbs, and please call me Spring."

An icy blast of air followed Shady in through the door. He glanced at the two of them, and cocked his head. "Did I miss something?"

"Nope, the lady just wants her space is all."

Shady with a big, boyish grin said, "Can't say that I blame you, ma'am. Bibbs isn't one for bathin' and the like."

Spring started to laugh but instantly stopped when she saw the hurt and anger in Bibbs' eyes. She'd hoped to feel safe here. Maybe all men had violence in them. Remembering Caleb, she knew she was wrong; he was a gentle soul.

"Spring?" Bibbs' gentle voice contrasted with his rugged exterior. "I didn't mean to scare you again. Truth told I'd love to crack an egg on this young'uns head, but I won't."

"I'm not a young'un." Shady smiled. "He's a big, old teddy bear. Hell, he even cries when his poor, old mama calls."

Spring glanced at Bibbs and relaxed at his smile. "I have a

31

few more things to add to the stew but you boys can set the table."

Bibbs nodded and grabbed some plates, and finally the tension seeped out of the house. Spring smiled when they fought about who sat where. This time she didn't feel fear, and it was a balm to her soul. Suddenly, the drafty house felt warm and cozy. Spring closed her eyes to cherish the feeling.

By the time she'd finished cooking, the table looked grand. Standing on her tiptoes, she tried to reach a bowl for the biscuits, but it was still just far enough away. She turned to grab a chair to stand on, but found herself in Bibbs' arms. He hoisted her up, waited until she grabbed the bowl and immediately set her down.

Spring smiled at him. Shady pegged him right, a big, old teddy bear. Spring pretended she didn't see Bibbs' face grow red. She simply thanked him and went back to stir the stew.

———

NO MATTER how many times he'd been through it, spring-time in Montana never ceased to amaze him. He never knew what type of weather to expect. The bitter cold and the howling wind were incessant. Colt patted Heavy Duty's neck. His poor horse's knee had started to swell about two miles out, and he'd walked him slowly and carefully toward home.

The snow came down hard and wet, clinging to his clothes, making them heavy. He wondered where his men were. Surely, they'd have noticed he hadn't come back yet. Hell, they probably thought he wanted to be alone. Colt tipped his Stetson lower to keep the snow out of his eyes, and a big pile of it fell off his hat as he did. They were close, he couldn't see the house lights yet, but he knew he would soon.

Trudging through the ankle deep snow was hard enough

for him, but poor Heavy Duty was really having a hard time of it. He hoped that he'd be able to bring down the swelling in the horse's knee. No way would a vet be able to make it out to the ranch, not in this weather.

He wondered how Spring was fairing. She would have been a nice addition to his little family, but he didn't want additions, not after losing Caleb. He couldn't mend his heart anymore. It'd been stitched together many times over the years, this time the stitches wouldn't hold.

Why did Rachael ask Caleb to find Snoopy? Where the hell was Stone or one of Stone's ranch hands? Why was Caleb the one who went searching for that mangy, oversized mutt? Pain lanced his heart. Stone and Winter never even came by the house, and they missed the funeral. "Damn you, McCoy!" His brow furrowed as his thoughts whirled through his head.

Every person he cared about had been stripped away from him leaving painful scars. He'd wait until better weather, until she'd had some time to get on her feet financially, and send Spring on her way. There was no happiness to be found on his ranch, and he didn't want her caught in the downfall of his hopes and dreams.

"Almost there, I can see the lights." His frozen lips barely got the words out to his horse.

Finally, he made it to the barn, fiddled at the latch with numb and shaking fingers and got the barn door opened. He hoped the landline worked. His cell hadn't been able to get a signal.

Walking Heavy Duty just outside his stall, he removed his saddle, wet saddle blanket, and fervently dried him with towels. Colt stopped briefly to call up to the house. It did something weird to his insides to hear Spring's voice answer. Bibbs and Shady were on their way out to help she said. He was tired, so cold and so tired.

Finally, they got Heavy Duty dry and his knee wrapped. Colt left the other two men to feed the rest of the horses while he hobbled toward the house. Every muscle was stiff and every bone chilled. He made it to the last step onto the porch, and the door opened. Immediately Spring put her arms around his waist and helped him inside.

He felt like a child, standing still while being undressed. He could have sworn he heard her mumbling about stubborn, stupid men but he didn't comment. It wasn't easy peeling off his heavy, wet clothes; he could see the strain on her face. When she finished with the outer layers, she led him to the rocking chair in front of the fireplace and helped him sit.

She briefly left, and for a moment, he felt lost without her until she returned with a heavy blanket and tucked it all around him. All he could think about was how good she smelled. He closed his eyes and began to feel the heat.

Soon, Spring was beside him again with a mug of coffee, which he gladly took from her. He looked past her and frowned at the doll on the counter.

He glanced at Spring and tried to hold back but it didn't work. "Where the hell did that doll come from?" Spring jumped high at his loud roar, but he didn't care. "How dare you! Where did you get that doll? Did it not occur to you that this is a house of mourning?"

Spring stepped back, her eyes wide. "Mr. McCoy brought it over."

"McCoy? McCoy was in my house? Tell me that I heard you wrong!"

Spring froze in place. She uttered not a word as she stared at him.

Quickly, he jumped out of the chair and grabbed the doll. He opened the door and flung the doll outside. It made a big thudding noise as it punched through the snow, but it didn't

34

make him any happier. He slammed the door shut and turned toward a horrified Spring. It tugged at his conscience a bit that she appeared so shaken up, but it was his house.

Breathing hard, he stomped back to the chair, grabbed his coffee and stared into the fire. Spring's frightened face gave him pause, but he decided what was done was done. She had no business accepting anything from McCoy. He watched her slowly walk to the stove. Her back was to him, but he could tell by the shaking of her shoulders she was upset.

Distress got to him every time. He was a sucker. Colt got up and walked toward Spring. The pot she stirred smelled delicious, and his stomach rumbled. Silently, he grabbed her hand, intending to lead her to the couch, but she whacked his arm with the wooden spoon she'd been using. "Whoa. That hurts." He instantly let go of her and went to the sink. Whatever she had in that pot of hers was hot.

"Here." She grabbed a towel, and turned the faucet on, wetting the towel. She threw the towel at him, shaking her head the whole while. "It looks worse than it probably feels."

"Now, why would you think that? It burns, and to my way of thinking it hurts as bad as it looks." He pulled his arm out of her grip.

Crossing her arms in front of her, she stared at him. "I always thought my injuries hurt as bad as it looked, worse even, but growing up I was always told to suck it up."

"Walk it off. I heard it often from my father."

She nodded. "I'm sorry I hit you, but you can't sneak up on a person and not expect consequences."

He blinked and cocked his head trying to figure out if she was apologizing or scolding. His lips twitched as he held out his hand. "This time I'll ask. Spring, would you like to sit down?"

She kept her arms folded. "No, I'm good. You still look a bit frozen, and you should go sit in front of the fire."

"I'm trying to apologize for upsetting you. I shouldn't have yelled at you."

"Don't give it a second thought." Her cool demeanor irritated him.

The oven timer buzzed, and she grabbed hot pads and opened the oven. She bent over, took the rolls out of the oven and put them on the counter. Glancing over her shoulder at him, her eyebrows knitted. "What's wrong?"

Her shirt had ridden up when she bent over, exposing her back. His eyes narrowed. "What happened to your back?" He walked to her side.

She stared at the rolls as if they fascinated her. After a bit, she sighed. "I'm fine." She turned and gave him a quick smile. "Let's get you back to that fire."

"Show me your back." He touched her hand.

She slowly took her hand from his. "This is one case where it looks worse than it hurts." Peering into his eyes, she shrugged. "You're not going to let this go are ya?"

"I'm afraid not."

"That's what I thought. One quick look and back to getting you dry."

He couldn't promise one quick look, and to hell with the fire. She lifted the back of her shirt, and he gasped seeing the fading bruises all up and down her back. Even her sides were bruised. Her skin was an ugly, painful mass of purple, green and brown.

"I'm fine. It doesn't hurt."

The front door opened, Shady and Bibbs entered laughing. One look across the room at Spring and Colt, and they both grew silent, their expressions morphing into shock and anger.

Bibbs was by her side before she could pull her shirt back down. "Someone kicked the tar out of you. It must hurt like the dickens, but you never let us know."

"I told Colt my shoulder hurt." Her voice was barely audible. "It's no big deal."

"Spring—" Colt started.

Before he could say another word, she ran to her room and closed the door behind her.

"Someone beat that poor little gal." Shady's fists clenched and unclenched.

Colt nodded. "That's probably why Caleb sent her out here. He wanted her safe."

"He sure did have a big heart."

"No big deal? Hell, if I had bruises like that it'd be a big deal." Colt stared at her closed door wondering how long she'd been with her ex.

———

SHE FELT, utterly mortified. The frightening way Colt dealt with the doll hardly registered. The shocked and sympathetic expressions on Shady and Bibb's faces became foremost in her mind.

It'd been embarrassing enough that Colt knew about her shoulder, but now he'd seen her disgusting body. She was never going to be any man's dream; she'd known that for a very long time. They would treat her differently now. They'd be careful of what they said and did. Everyone would be walking on eggshells around her.

Her heart beat faster, thinking about the expression on Colt's face. All her synapses were firing at once, and she'd become overloaded with emotion. When he said he didn't look at her when her towel flew off, he must have told the truth.

If she'd had a proper coat and boots, she'd be out the door so fast. She wanted to go to the barn and see the horses. Bibbs mentioned something about abused horses, and she wondered if they felt the same way she did, skittish one minute and ready to fight the next.

Her bedroom door began to open, and Spring felt a huge lump form in her throat. She had to look calm no matter how much she screamed inside. Swallowing hard, she clasped her hands on her lap, and sat on the bed, ever mindful of being still.

She'd been prepared for anger. Instead, Colt gave her a sheepish look. She didn't know what to think.

He closed the door behind him, causing her to stiffen.

"I'm sorry, I shouldn't have pried but those bruises would have kept anyone else in bed. They took me by surprise, and I sure didn't expect Shady and Bibbs to walk in. I'm pretty much known as a nice guy, but I haven't given you any reason to think that." He sighed heavily.

His stare bore holes into her, and she wasn't sure what to say. "It's not you. I'm not good with people. I try but… I like to keep my life private is all."

Colt shuffled his feet a bit. "I don't know how to be around women. I mean I've never really lived with one and with you being hurt and all."

"I hear you take in rescue horses."

"Yes I do. Most of them have been abused. I guess I need to take a page out of my own book, and treat you with gentleness. I mean, I know you're not a horse or anything." His face turned red, and he jammed his hands in his jeans pockets.

Spring gave him a brief smile. "I'm just jumpy is all. I'm fine."

Colt's eyes widened a bit, and she could tell he wasn't buying it. "You have reason to be jumpy. I know you're embarrassed Bibbs and Shady found out, but I find it's best to be aware of what we're dealing with, how to handle things."

"Handle things?"

Colt shuffled his feet again. "There I go treating you like a scared filly. Dang, I'm no good at talking to women anymore. Anyway, I'll go bring the doll back in."

"Her name is Faith."

Colt sighed. "I know Caleb gave it to Rachael. That pie, you didn't make it did you?"

"No."

Colt nodded and grabbed the doorknob. "Can you make cookies?"

Spring nodded.

"There then that's all that's needed. I don't want any pie." Colt left the room leaving the door open.

Spring sighed. Maybe it would be all right after all. She could hope.

CHAPTER FOUR

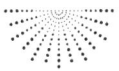

*A*fter breakfast the next morning, Spring busied herself making fudge. The smell of chocolate permeated the air. Smiling, she looked down at the new red sweater and turtleneck she found waiting for her this morning. Somehow, the drafty house didn't seem as cold anymore.

Colt was certainly a mystery. He didn't know it was her birthday, and he waved her "thank you" away. She could tell he was embarrassed, so she left him alone but she wanted to tell him they were the best birthday gifts she ever had.

Bibbs and Shady were a completely different story. They treated her like a china doll until she had to yell at them. All morning it was "thank you, ma'am", "can I help you, ma'am". Finally, she had to tell them that too much niceness could get on one's nerves.

Shaking her head, she remembered their surprised and puzzled expressions. She'd been ready for a few stares this morning but a total change had been too much. She thought of Caleb, and how he never treated her differently after he knew about the fights she and Billy had. She missed him. Colt must be going through hell. She knew all about loss and heartbreak, and her heart squeezed. She needed to be more aware of his feelings.

The last batch of fudge was ready and cornbread was in the oven. She gave the chili a quick stir and put the coffee on. Almost lunch time. Those three could sure put back a lot of food, but she didn't mind. She was starting to like having the company, and she hoped things would go back to the way they were.

The sound of heavy boots stomping on the front porch alerted her to their arrival. Quickly, she poured the coffee and put the mugs on the old wooden table.

"Smells good in here." Colt grabbed a piece of fudge from a plate and popped it into his mouth.

Spring turned and slapped his hand. She instantly realized her mistake. It was one thing to fight back but starting the fight never boded well. The last time she slapped Billy, he slapped her in return, so hard that her ears rang.

"Can't decide which smells better, the fudge or the chili." His chocolate eyes gentled.

Spring's heartbeat started to slow from pounding painfully against her ribcage. How long and what would it take her to react like a normal person? "Maybe it's the cornbread." Her voice squeaked, reminding her of a frog.

Shady sat down at the table and drank his coffee, smiling at her.

"What are you smiling at?" Colt sat down and raised his eyebrows at Shady.

"Cornbread of course." Shady grinned at Colt. "I would smile at the pretty lady, but I have a feeling I'd get my butt kicked if I did."

Bibbs laughed. "I like cornbread too."

Spring didn't know what was going on between the men and didn't care to know. She grabbed the cornbread out of the oven and cut it into pieces. Grabbing three heavy, chipped bowls, she ladled chili into each, setting them out on the table with a couple hunks of cornbread apiece. Sitting at the table with her own bowl, she looked at each man in turn. Shady and Bibbs kept shifting their gaze from her to Colt and back again. Did they think she was sweet on Colt? She wasn't sure if they even had one brain between them.

"Good chili, Miss Spring." Bibbs nodded at her.

"Thank you. I kept it to a medium."

"It's a far sight better than what we make. Ain't it, Colt?"

Colt nodded. "Bibbs is right. We usually just eat canned stuff."

Spring felt a glow at his praise.

"Glad ole Caleb sent her to us."

Both Spring and Colt stopped eating. Shady kept eating not realizing that he had touched a sore spot. Spring looked into Colt's eyes and saw his misery, and she wished she could take his anguish away. Maybe she made it worse by being there. Biting her bottom lip, she glanced away. There wasn't any help for it. Until the snow stopped, she was stuck. Biting her lip harder, she reminded herself that it wasn't the snow, she was just plain stuck.

Shady and Bibbs got up, thanked her and left. Colt lingered at the table watching her clean up. His stare made her so aware of him in such a different way than she'd been aware of any other man. She felt nervous and tingly all at once.

Drying her hands, she walked toward the table. "I shouldn't have accepted the pie and doll. I can see it makes you sad, and I don't want to be the cause of your misery."

"Oh, sugar, you're not." Colt took her hand and gave it a gentle squeeze. "I don't know how I'd get through this if not for you. Your being here helps more than you could ever know."

Gladness flowed into her heart. It really was a sad time,

but his presence helped her too. Her soul felt less troubled, and some of the weight had left her shoulders.

Colt let go of her hand and stood up. He gazed at her with his big, brown eyes, smiling at her, and this time his smile reached his eyes. He didn't move, just stared until finally he winked at her and walked toward the door. Grabbing his outdoor clothing, he left.

Spring stood there for a long while, cherishing the moment they just shared. She couldn't remember the last time someone winked at her. What was it supposed to mean?

Shaking her head, she continued with her baking until there was a knock on the door. Who'd be out in this weather she couldn't imagine. She hurried to the door and opened it, shocked to see Stone McCoy standing on the other side.

"Winter and Rachael wanted to talk to Colt." Stone's eyes were wretched.

Spring quickly opened the door wider to let in all of them. They all looked upset and cold.

"This is my wife, Winter and our daughter Rachael."

Spring nodded at each. She felt immediately drawn to the little girl wearing a green hat with little brown curls escaping from it. Misery emanated from her.

"Nice to meet you, I'm Spring. Come in and get warm." Spring ushered them in toward the big fireplace. "Have a seat, I'll get you something warm to drink, and for heaven's sake take off those wet clothes."

She didn't know what to think. How was Colt going to react to them being here? Badly for sure. She quickly poured some coffee and made some hot chocolate. The house was silent. No one spoke.

"Here we go. Coffee for the adults and hot chocolate for Rachael." Spring handed out the drinks and brought over milk and sugar. Sitting down, she wondered how long it would be until Colt got back.

Winter started to cry then Rachael joined in. Startled, Spring jumped up and grabbed a box of tissues for the two. Not knowing how to deal with all the sudden emotion, she just numbly sat back down.

"I'm sorry." Winter tried to give her a brief smile as her tears subsided. "Stone told me that you were a friend of Caleb's."

"I met him not too long ago. He'd come into the diner where I worked almost every night. He'd study, and I'd bring him coffee. I was having some trouble, and he offered me a job here. I guess we all cared about him."

"Look, Mama, the house looks really clean."

"It surely shines in here." Winter turned toward Spring. "Rachael insisted that her daddy bring over her doll."

Spring was getting ready to say something nice when the door swung open.

"What the hell? I couldn't believe it when I saw your truck outside." Colt didn't acknowledge the women he just stomped toward Stone.

His fists were clenched, and his face was full of pain. She was afraid that he'd take a swing at Stone.

Rachael got up and ran to Colt. Wrapping her arms around his legs, she began to sob, heart-breaking sobs. His anger dissolving, Colt reached down and lifted her into his big arms. He pulled her close and whispered to her.

Spring felt a tear trail down her face. Hastily she grabbed a tissue and wiped it away.

"It's all my fault! I kilted Caleb!" Rachael wrapped her tiny arms around Colt's neck and held on tight.

Colt's eyes closed, and his face grew grim. When he opened his eyes, he sought her out. The pain there was almost too much to bear. His eyes began to soften as Rachael kissed his cheek. He walked to the couch and sat with the little girl in his lap.

"Colt, I'm so sorry. I didn't know... When Snoopy came up missing, I told Rachael it was too dangerous to go looking for him in the storm."

Colt swallowed hard and gave her a curt nod. "It was an accident, and Rachel's not to blame. I'm just surprised she had use of a phone."

Winter's face grew red. "I'm so sorry, Colt. I...I wasn't aware she'd called Caleb until he showed up with Snoopy. Stone was out of town, and I couldn't bring myself to face you. We missed Caleb's funeral, and I'm deeply sorry."

"I'll send Snoopy away if you want," Rachael bravely told him. Her chin wobbled while she waited for Colt's answer.

"No, Snoopy isn't at fault either. Now Caleb's in heaven with God."

"Like an angel?"

Colt smiled a real smile, albeit a sad one. "Like an angel."

Stone shot Colt a thankful look. "You've been family to us and..."

Colt took a deep breath and pressed his lips together. "Still am and..." He looked around as though he was searching for something to say until his gaze met Spring's. "Spring was a friend of Caleb's."

Winter stood and sat next to Spring, hugging her. She couldn't remember the last time she had a female friend. Billy had always warned her friends away; in fact, Billy had warned everyone away.

Her spirit lightened as an understanding flowed between Colt and the McCoys. Colt still looked haunted but he didn't look as old. Perhaps some of his burden lightened.

After a great deal of tears and hugs, Rachael got her doll back, and the McCoys left. The house became silent, too silent.

"I'll start some dinner. I'm sure that Bibbs and Shady will be hungry. It's starting to get dark." Walking away from him, she felt like a blithering idiot, but the silence needed to be filled. "Tomorrow is Sunday. Are we still snowed in? Do you go to church? I never had much opportunity for church going."

"I have something to show you outside."

"It's too cold."

"Not if you wear boots and a coat."

Spring turned toward him. "But—"

"Look over at the coat rack."

Spring didn't want to look away from his eyes. It wasn't often he looked happy, and she didn't want to see it disappear, but she did what he asked and ran over to the pegged coat rack. A new, midnight blue winter coat hung from one of the pegs. She touched it, running her hands over the faux fur around the hood. Looking down she saw a tan pair of boots that looked like those beautiful boots from Australia that everyone else seemed to have. The sweater she'd received earlier in the day had touched her but this; it was the nicest gift she'd ever received.

Turning, she looked at Colt. He looked pleased. "They're new."

"Yes, they are, and they're yours."

Spring took the coat down and ran her hands over the soft fleece lining. Brushing the faux black fur against her face made her sigh. She laid it carefully on the worn wooden bench beneath the pegs, reached down and picked up the boots. Sitting on the bench, she examined every aspect of them right down to the stitching. Looking up, she smiled at Colt. "They're in my size."

"Of course they are. Bibbs is a fine detective when he wants to be. He looked at the label in your jacket and checked your shoes for the size. Hurry put them on we don't want to miss it."

The urgency in his voice spurred her on. She wanted to

look in the mirror but Colt started tapping his foot to spur her on. Grabbing her hand, he pulled her out the door and led her to a path in the snow.

"What is it?"

"You'll see. We'll be there in a minute."

The walk was mostly uphill but Spring had a suspicion the strain on her legs would be worth it. She was warm and grateful for it. Darkness began to fall just as they reached the top. Spring gasped. The colors of the magnificent, heaven-sent sunset left her speechless. Rich hues of pink and purples mixed with orange and blue stopped her in her tracks.

"Worth the walk?"

"Oh yes. Thank you for sharing this with me." A wide smile spread across her face.

"It's a sight I never get used to. It's different every day and every season."

Staring at his strong profile, her smile deepened. "I didn't realize that your land is nestled by mountains. I could see the mountain tops from the house, but I thought they were further away."

"This land has been in my family since the Homestead Act of 1862. The ranch was started with 160 acres, and now is a little over 600 acres. The land is worth more than the cattle but it's in my blood. Times might be a bit lean now but that's just how it goes. There are good years, and there are years I struggle to hold on."

"Your family would have been proud."

Colt gave her a sad smile. "I was holding on for Caleb. I figured he'd have a family of his own to pass it all down to. Now, I just don't know."

Spring sidestepped, closing the gap between them, allowing her shoulder to press gently against his arm. She hoped to offer comfort, but she just didn't know if she succeeded. They stood there and watched the sun disappear.

It grew colder, but she didn't want to disturb the silence by asking to go in.

"You're shaking." The concern in his voice touched her.

"Just a bit. I'd be shaking much more so if you hadn't bought me this coat and these boots. Thank you. I've never had new boots before, or a coat. I've never had the time or inclination to watch the sunset either, and I never knew the beauty of it."

"You are more than welcome." Colt reached for her hand, and she automatically put distance between them as they walked down the hill. "Sandwiches will be fine for dinner since you haven't had time for anything else. We're used to them."

"Looks like the boys are already home. Yes, sandwiches are quick. Thank you again." Before Colt had a chance to reply, she quickly opened the door and greeted Bibbs and Shady.

All throughout dinner, Colt studied her until she turned bright red from the attention. At one point, she wondered if she had a piece of food on her face. It made her uncomfortable, and her stomach fluttered.

He certainly was a contrary man. One minute mad as all get out, and then tender the next. The last few days had their difficulties, but she was certain he had a good heart and it was something she could carry with her through the doubt. Now if he would stop staring at her, they might have a nice dinner.

Shady and Bibbs kept exchanging glances, and it made her wonder. She felt Caleb's absence keenly in moments like these. He'd been such a friend to her and would have been the one she could speak to in this sea of looks. It was still hard to believe that he was gone. Whatever she felt she knew Colt felt it tenfold.

She served them cake for dessert since it was her birthday. Even though no one knew, she'd had the best birthday ever.

After dinner, Colt excused himself and went out to the barn. Bibbs and Shady said their "goodnights" and went to the hardly-used bunkhouse. Then the house was quiet, almost too quiet. Colt had been so good to her. Tomorrow she'd make cookies for him as a thank you for the coat and boots. He'd already given her so much she didn't expect more. Colt, Bibbs and Shady had all treated her with respect but she couldn't help but be on alert in case of trouble, in case this kindness melted away. What was it like to simply be able to relax and enjoy?

She waited a while for Colt to return but he stayed in the barn. She could see the lights on across the way. Finally, she gave in and went to bed. She rolled onto her right side trying to get comfortable and winced. Her shoulder still hurt like hell. Maybe she'd get a chance to heal. She couldn't remember the last time her whole body was bruise free.

COLT LEANED against the barn door waiting for the house lights to go off. He was a coward, but he couldn't deal with the feelings that Spring brought to the surface. Women weren't his forte, but Spring was different. She reminded him of his poor mistreated horses, and he'd have to be gentle with her. He wished he could fist plant the guy responsible.

Gazing at the house, he wondered what type of life she'd led. It was bad enough for Caleb to help her get away from her ex-boyfriend. The light in her bedroom went off, and taking a deep breath, he headed toward the house.

At least McCoy finally came over and explained things. Poor little Rachael's cries tore his heart, and Winter's guilt floored him. His pain had overridden his judgment in dealing with the McCoys. He still harbored a little resentment, but some of his anger finally drained after they left. A weight lifted from his shoulders and he was grateful. It had become almost too much to bear.

Rachael was such a special girl, offering to get rid of Snoopy. She loved Caleb too. He thought back to the Winter Dance, smiling as he remembered Rachael yelling, "dip me!" to Caleb. They'd had a special bond. One time Rachael came to spend the night, and she slid down the porch banister, landing face first onto the hard, frozen snow. The only one who she'd take comfort from was Caleb.

He took off his coat and hung it up next to Spring's. He smiled remembering her excitement over her new coat and boots. Her blue eyes brightened his day, perhaps a bit too much. He had a right to still mourn, he had a right to be angry, and he had a right to hell… he didn't know.

He liked her too much and that couldn't happen. It was never his plan and never his dream. These days he just wanted to work with his horses and be left alone. Caleb hired her so he'd honor Caleb's decision but that was as far as it could go. No more walks together. They would just be employer and employee.

She was a little bit of a thing, and whoever hurt her was a fool. First of all, you never hit a woman, let alone pick on someone so small. He must have beaten the tar out of her. He was glad Caleb gave her the job, but that was Caleb's way, kind and generous. His heart hurt again as he headed for bed. Tomorrow was another day, and it would be filled with the same pain as today. The first thought of his day would be *Caleb is dead.* His heart would plummet and his stomach would be in knots. He'd lay there for a moment wishing it wasn't so. He'd bargain with God to bring Caleb back even though he knew it wasn't possible. He'd force himself to get up and live. The horses needed him and now it seemed as though Spring needed him too.

COLT HAD ALREADY LEFT by the time she woke up. Disappointment filled her to the point she thought herself crazy. She'd only known him a few days. The coffee was already made, so she poured herself a cup and glanced out the window at the barn. How could she miss someone she barely knew?

Cookies were on her agenda for today as well as finding a cookbook. Bibbs had brought a turkey home with the groceries the other day, and she needed to figure out how to cook it. She turned the radio on and switched stations until she found Country music, singing along as she baked. Soon enough it was lunchtime and still no Colt. Now she began to feel guilty. Somehow she'd run him out of his own house.

He probably figured she had designs on him. If he only knew of her fear of men—well most men. They had the physical power to hurt a woman, regardless of what she did to defend herself, and she'd learned that lesson all her life. Caleb had been her first male friend, and he turned into the voice of reason she'd needed.

It had cost her to leave Texas, but now she felt as though she could breathe. Snow was falling as she put on her new coat and boots and headed outside. It was glorious as it floated through the air. Some clumped on her eyelashes, and she could feel it on her hair. She stood there in the middle of the yard enjoying the fresh wind chilling her cheeks. The wind stung but she felt a sense of freedom she'd lost long ago.

The barn beckoned her. It might not be the wisest choice

but she wanted to see the horses. Colt may be in there, but it was a chance she'd take.

The door was heavier than she'd thought, but she managed to get it open and immediately the musty, manure smell assaulted her. It would take some getting used to.

It was bigger than she expected and warmer. Stalls on each side of the building seem to go on forever. A horse poked his head over the stall door nearest to her, and she yelped in surprise, quickly covering her mouth. She didn't want to startle any of the horses.

Colt peeked out from one of the stalls. He appeared puzzled then he broke out in a wide grin. "Looking for me?"

The beating of her heart became louder. "No, not really." She turned toward the horse and was horrified to see it so close with its mouth open. She jumped back. "He's trying to bite me!"

The laughter was deep. Colt shook his head. "Nope, Hurricane likes hats and hair. He doesn't bite."

"He likes hair?"

"He's been known to nibble on locks of hair. He doesn't pull it out or anything. He just gets it good and wet."

Quickly, she stepped back even further. "Is that why you had to rescue him?"

Colt's smile dimmed. "No, if you look closely there are whip marks on him. His owner wasn't the nicest of men."

"Oh my."

"He's in good hands now."

Sympathy for Hurricane filled her. She knew what it was like to be beaten. "I'm glad he has you to look after him."

Colt nodded and started to hold his hand out to her but jammed them in his pockets instead. "Come with me, I have someone for you to meet." He led her down the row of stalls, stopping at the one he just came from. "Look."

She'd never seen a real horse let alone a newborn. A foal

was nursing while its mother looked on. They were both brown with black manes. "That's the most beautiful thing I've ever seen. Look, Colt, look at the baby nursing. The mare is feeding her just like a mother would."

"Exactly how a good mother would." His voice trailed off at the end.

She stared at the mare. She often wished for a good mother.

"Is it a boy or girl?"

"That's a colt, a male. A female would be a filly."

Her smile grew wider; she couldn't help herself. "This so exciting. Did you help?"

Colt stared at the horses. "Yes, the mare needed a little help."

"Wow. That's amazing. What are their names?"

"The mare is Heidi. The little guy doesn't have a name yet." He gave her a sidelong glance. "Would you like to name him?"

Spring's heart flipped over in her chest. "Really?"
"Sure."

Her mind went blank. It should be a good name, a noble name. The sudden responsibility overwhelmed her. "I don't know what to name him. What do people name horses?"

He grinned at her, and she wondered if she sounded like a moron. "Anything you want, sugar."

"How about Daybreak? Kind of like a new beginning."

"You know I like that. That's what's needed, a new beginning. Might not be today or tomorrow even but eventually I'll be ready for a new beginning." Colt's smile was contagious, and she smiled back.

It was as if something passed between them, and it was a nice feeling she'd never experienced before. They watched Daybreak and Heidi for a bit more. Spring didn't know what else to say. It was an easy silence, yet she thought she should be saying something.

"I'm going back to the house." She turned and peered up at him. "Will you be home for dinner?"

His smile changed, and she didn't know how to read it. He nodded.

Walking back to the house, she wondered what it all meant. He was a changeable one. He acted kind and glad to be around her, yet she sensed a reluctance to interact with her. It didn't matter, not really. As long as she worked hard, she'd be fine.

She opened the door and was met by an appalling sight. There stood Bibbs and Shady, stuffing her cookies in their mouths. The amount already missing from the plate made her heart drop. "Well from the amount of cookies gone, I guess you don't want dinner." She took her coat and boots off and stood at the edge of the kitchen with her hands on her hips.

Bibbs at least had the good sense to look guilty. Shady just gave her a grin with his mouth full.

"Ma'am, I apologize. I haven't had a home-baked cookie in years. These were so good, I just couldn't help myself."

"I see." She turned to Shady. "What's your excuse?"

"Well, you see, Bibbs here thought he smelled cookies, and he had a hankering for some. We came inside, and here they were like a gift from those little green elves. I mean what are the odds? We think about cookies and here they are."

The more she got to know Shady, the more off she thought he was. "I'm supposed to believe that you thought elves brought you cookies?"

She felt a cold chill at her back and then a rumble of laughter. "I could have come up with something better, Shady. Elves?"

She turned and gazed at Colt. The laughter reached his eyes, and she was glad. "Not just any elves. They were apparently green elves."

Colt roared with laughter. He walked over to the cookies, and helped himself to one. "They do look mighty fine." He took a bite and nodded. "Yes, Shady is right. These taste the same as the other ones the green elves left for us a few years back."

Spring grabbed a kitchen towel and threw it at Colt. He stopped laughing and for an instant, she thought she'd done something wrong. She braced herself but all she got was another round of laughter.

After dinner, Shady and Bibbs left. Spring washed the dishes while trying to keep an eye on Colt. During dinner, they were all kidding around until Shady mentioned Caleb again. Now Colt stared morosely at the fire with his shoulders hunched over, and his expression spoke of immense pain. It hurt her heart to watch him. He was so nice and so was Caleb. It must be devastating to lose a brother but she really had no reference. She never had a family. She thought she did once, she thought her and Billy would be a family. Now she was glad she'd been made to see the truth about him before she'd gotten pregnant. Thank God for Caleb.

Billy had wanted them to have kids, but now she realized he never mentioned marriage. Somehow, it never came up. Wouldn't a couple trying to have children have at least talked about marriage or a future? Maybe their brains were wired differently because of their upbringing.

That's what brought them together in the first place. They both had no one except each other. It had been a hard existence, and Billy protected her from the other boys at the last home she had lived. She never had protection before, not from the boys or from anyone. She'd thought of Billy as her savior, but she learned the hard way he wasn't.

Strange, he never showed any sign of his aggression until they had both aged out of the foster care system. Billy's birthday was first, and he'd found a rundown apartment and a job driving a delivery truck. She'd thought they'd hit the big time. When she aged out, she went to live with him. Immediately she got the job at the diner, and soon after, he started to beat her.

Thank God, for Caleb, otherwise she'd still be with Billy. By the time she'd left, the beatings had accelerated but he'd never hit her face before. She left Texas two weeks after Caleb. He'd given her a bus ticket. She snuck out in the dead of night like a fugitive, but she did it, she escaped. Colt didn't know what a blessing he and his ranch were to her.

It physically hurt to see Colt so sad. She closed the gap between them and laid her hand on his strong shoulder. He placed his hand over hers, giving it a squeeze. Turning his head, he gave her a wilted smile.

"Just thinking I guess."

She gave him a brief smile. "It's fine. I know you have a lot on your mind. It must be so hard for you. You're mourning, I understand."

Colt let go of her hand and patted the cushion next to him. She sat down on the couch. "What are some of your favorite family memories?" he asked.

She took a deep breath. "I guess I never really told you much about me."

"You don't have to." His gentle voice was almost too much.

"I want you to know. We're friends after all. I come from nothing. I grew up in a slew of foster homes, some not good, and some even worse."

"Why weren't you adopted?"

She shrugged her shoulder. "My mother wouldn't give up her rights to me. There was no way she could have me. She was always chasing after her next high, and they all knew she'd never be fit, but I wasn't adoptable." She stared into the fire to avoid seeing any pity in his eyes.

"Sounds like a hard life."

"You have problems of your own. You don't need to add to your burden by worrying about me."

"I don't see how you'd ever be a burden."

Spring turned toward him, trying to see if he was being honest. "I've always been a burden. At least here, I'm working to pay my way. It's my choice for once."

Silence ensued; she wondered if she should ask him about his favorite memories. It might open his wounds, and she didn't want to add to his pain.

"You said a slew of homes. How many did you live in?"

Taking a deep breath, she closed her eyes. Slowly she let her breath out. "I think about nine. Well actually ten but one I only stayed a couple of hours. The woman claimed I was too enticing to be around her husband. Just as well, he probably would have come to me in the dead of night."

"Really?"

"Yes, really. Unfortunately, just like everything, there are good and bad. I loved the good places but they never seemed to last very long. Kids were always bounced from home to home. There never seemed to be a set reason. Sometimes it was the parents, who didn't want you in their homes, or it was the social worker, and they never gave you a reason. One perceived misstep could land you in a tougher home. It was hard moving from school to school but the worst part was not knowing when they would move you again."

"Tougher homes?"

She nodded. "Yes, the homes where they put hard-to-place troublemakers. The kids, who lied, stole, assaulted others and were one-step away from juvie. It didn't matter if you were actually guilty of any of the infractions or not. I've never really had anything that belonged just to me. Everyone helped themselves to my clothes. I wore what no one else wanted. That's just the way it was. That's why the sweater, hat and boots you bought me mean so much. I know they are mine to keep."

"Caleb and I never had much but what we did have was ours to keep. Our mother died when we were young, and our son of a bitch father raised us until his heart gave out. He was too busy being bitter at the world to be much of a father. I'm never going to love anyone the way he loved my mother. It ruined my father's life when she died. He never got over it, and I believe it's why he died so young. I was twenty-one, and Caleb was sixteen. He was the smart one, and he won a full scholarship to college but he almost didn't go. He didn't want to leave Montana and go to Texas, but I made him go. He was happy once he got there."

Spring put her head on his shoulder. "He seemed happy enough. I don't think he had much of a social life. He spent most of his time studying. He did mention you a time or two. He wanted to make you proud, but when he was done with his schooling he was heading for home for good."

"That's Caleb. He hated that I had to shoulder so much responsibility. I told him his responsibility was to learn as much as he could and bring his knowledge home."

His body began to shake. Spring lifted her head and put her arms around his shoulders, awkwardly hugging him. His tremors went straight through her. She whispered words of comfort to him, and after a moment, he stilled and pulled away.

"If this is too hard for you, Colt, we don't have to talk." She studied his brown eyes trying to gauge his feelings, but he hid them well.

"Actually it's the first time that I've been able to talk about him. It hurt too much before, and I was so damn angry. It helps to have you here."

She'd been through hell in her life, but all her concern right now was for Colt. Life hadn't been fair for either one of them. She could tell that he was a survivor just like her. That knowledge made her feel good inside. She didn't know what the future held for either of them, but she knew that they would be friends.

They sat in silence for a while. Standing, she leaned over and patted his shoulder. "Good night, Colt."

He gave her a brief smile. "Good night, Spring."

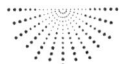

CHAPTER FIVE

*C*olt ran his hand over his freshly shaven face. Morning came early. He had a hard time getting to sleep but when he finally did sleep, it was the most peaceful slumber he'd had since Caleb's death. He was sure word had gotten out around town that he had someone looking after him, because no one had tried to push a casserole on him since Spring arrived.

The snow lessened yesterday, so most of the roads were passable. Bibbs and Shady could go home today if they wanted. He had a suspicion they'd just stay around hoping for some of Spring's cooking. She seemed to know her way around the kitchen, and his house had never looked cleaner. Pulling on a green flannel shirt, he made his way downstairs.

Spring must have already been up. He could smell the coffee as he approached the kitchen.

She stood near the stove looking at the timer, turning as he entered the room. Her blue eyes lit up. With long red hair draped over her shoulders, she was an attractive little thing. He watched as she poured him his coffee and brought it over. "Thank you."

She smiled and nodded, hurrying back to the stove.

"What you got cookin'? It smells wonderful."

"It's a chocolate cake. I never made a cake before so I'm a bit anxious." She lifted the cookbook from the counter and showed it to him.

"I've used that book many a time. After ma died, my dad was too depressed to eat much, let alone cook for Caleb and me. I got out the cookbook, and it became my kitchen bible."

Her smile lit up the room. "I found it the other day. I can cook but I need a recipe. Sit, I'll make you some breakfast."

He sat and watched as she whipped up bacon, eggs and toast, enjoying the view in the meantime. Her rear end swayed back and forth while she cooked. It was the perfect shape, and he suddenly had the notion to squeeze it. He wondered what it would be like to have her under him, open to him as he drove into her. He willed himself to pull his gaze away. It wouldn't do thinking like that.

He remembered his father, and the pain he suffered when his mother died. He remembered the suffering he and Caleb had. No, women weren't for him. He refused to put his happiness in someone else's hands again. He suddenly felt uncomfortable sitting at the kitchen table. To his relief, Bibbs and Shady came blustering in the door right then.

"Close the door!"

Bibbs looked at him and smiled. "I know, I know, we don't have to try to heat the whole world with your tiny furnace."

They took off their coats and both approached Spring. Shady handed her a brown paper bag stapled closed at the top. This is from us. Happy Birthday."

She gasped, and her face turned red. "For me?" Her expression was one of bewilderment. She handed the spatula to Shady and sat at the table. With trembling hands, she opened the package. Reaching in, she pulled out a matching set of blue gloves and hat. Tears came to her eyes, and she tried to smile.

Bibbs frowned. "If you don't like it, we can take it back and get you something else. Shady and I are no good at buying woman things."

Spring wiped away a stray tear. "No. They are lovely, and I'll treasure them always."

Bibbs sighed in relief. "Good. They match your coat. Shady and I got them when we got your coat and boots from the store. Did you notice that everything matches? That was my idea."

Shady shook his head. "I was the one that came up with the matching part, Spring. If you must know, I've suspected that old Bibbs here is color blind."

Bibbs face colored and irritation emanated from him. Spring put her hand on Bibbs' arm as she stood and kissed his cheek. "Thank you."

She walked over to Shady, took the spatula out of his hand and kissed his cheek too. "Thank you. How did you know yesterday was my birthday?"

Shady shifted his weight back and forth. "I guess the elves told me?"

"Oh hell, Shady saw your driver's license but he got the day wrong." Bibbs looked embarrassed by the whole thing.

Spring nodded. "I guess I did have it out the other day. I wanted to see if I could keep this one or if I needed to get a Montana one. It doesn't matter at all about the date. I think I'm starting to like you two."

Shady's eye widened. "Starting?"

Spring got busy and made them breakfast, and Colt had never seen her look so happy. It made him proud she considered necessities treasures. She sure was different from others he'd known.

Between Shady insisting he didn't know how he got the

day wrong, and Bibbs muttering about stupid people, breakfast was lovely.

"Bibbs, you and Shady clean the kitchen. I want to show Spring my gift."

"You already gave me this red sweater, the coat and boots. Truly I don't need anything else."

"You are pretty as a picture. Come on get your gear on we're going for a walk."

She nodded and was ready to go in record time. Colt held the door open for her. He could hear Bibbs mumbling about closing the door and heating the whole world. Colt smiled. He grabbed her hand and led her to the barn. Quickly opening the door, he drew her inside and walked down to Heidi and Daybreak's stall. He expected her to snatch her hand back, but she didn't.

"They are as cute as could be."

Colt gazed at her. "Yep, the cutest ever."

Spring peered at him, and her eyes widened as she realized that he wasn't talking about the horses.

"I want you to have Daybreak. Of course that means we'll have to adopt Heidi too, but it'll be worth it so they can stay together."

"You're giving me a horse?"

Colt nodded. He'd given many horses away in his life, but he'd never seen the expression Spring wore, an expression of sheer delight that ran deep. Part of him wished that he could always make her so happy.

"To keep?"

Colt nodded.

"Forever?"

"Yes of course, honey."

Spring stood on tiptoe and quickly kissed him square on the lips. She suddenly jumped away. "I'm sorry! I, well thank you."

Their gazes locked. Something passed between them. He wasn't sure what, but it felt good.

"I'd better get the house clean and some laundry done. A lot needs to be done."

"You shouldn't have to clean all the time. I need to make time to teach you how to keep the books. I haven't touched them since..."

She smiled. "I'm just grateful to have a place."

"You go on in. I need to work with these horses."

She hesitated. "Do you think that someday you could teach me about horses?"

The heaviness in his heart lightened a bit. "Sure, honey, I'd be delighted."

A WEEK LATER, the roads had finally cleared, and the snow was melting as temperatures finally started to climb. Spring enjoyed the milder weather. It reminded her of the warmth that was probably already in the air back home.

She still did all the housework and cooking, but she found time every afternoon to join Colt in the barn. Most of the time they were alone. Daybreak had come to know her and came right to her. She loved that little foal. Soon she learned that her foal was a quarter horse, a bay quarter horse to be exact. His coloring was that of his mother's.

Pulling on her coat, she walked to the barn. The warmer air stroked her face differently. She didn't miss the biting cold as the new season rolled in.

Inside she spied Colt talking to Yokel as he slowly approached him. The poor horse had been neglected for so long; Colt had to cut the halter off his head. The paint was terrified of other horses, only allowing Colt in the same stall with him. She sat back and admired his way with them.

He noticed her standing there and winked. "I'd love to have just one minute with his owner."

"I know. You have a very caring way with them, and they are lucky to have you." She walked toward him down the length of the barn.

He shrugged his shoulders. "I always had a way with horses. Don't know what I do differently than anyone else. I'm trying to get Yokel to let me touch him without flinching."

"Must be hard when you find them homes."

"Some more than others. Yokel here will be a challenge. He refuses to allow anyone to lead him out of the stall. I put him in the birthing stall to work with him. It gives us more room." He let himself out of the stall and locked the door. Leaning against it, he smiled. "It's that whole double edge sword thing. I'm a proud papa when they learn and get better. I'm also sad to see them go. I make sure they go to good homes, but there are a few I'll never be able to find homes for. Like Sideways here." He pointed to a black horse.

"Why what's wrong with Sideways?"

"He's blind and his best friend is Squirt. Squirt is a chestnut pony. He's Sideways' eyes. It's amazing to see them together. Sideways is fine here, he's gotten used to it. I did try to take them both out to a ranch to be fostered. But Sideways stopped eating."

"I thought this was ranch country. Why so many hurt horses?"

"Hurt? That's being polite. Most of the horses are abused, neglected, starved. It's lucky that I refuse to get a horse if the owner is on the property. I just might have to kill one or two. There are other reasons too. Hay prices are tripling, and the job market sucks."

He appeared troubled, and she couldn't blame him. "They really are lucky to have you."

Colt gazed at her and grinned. "You're going to make my head too big to fit my hat, talking that way."

She pretended to look at Squirt, but she actually had Colt in her sights. He was a good man, just like Caleb, and she was lucky to have him. Well, she didn't really have him, but being near him gave her a sense of security. Colt turned back and caught her staring, and she turned red. It wouldn't do her any favors to keep thinking that way. He already said he didn't want a woman.

"I'm going to look in on Daybreak and Heidi then I have dinner to make."

"Anything good?" His boyish grin enchanted her.

"Pot roast."

"That's my favorite," Bibbs said, walking into the barn.

Spring laughed. "Every meal is your favorite."

"That it is." He glanced at Colt. "You might want to snatch her before someone else does."

Colt's embarrassment was evident. "I'm going back to start dinner." Quickly, she left the barn. Even though she didn't have any delusions about her future with him, she didn't want to hear Colt's rejection either.

There was a box on the front porch. As she got closer, she spied her name on it. A lump formed in her throat. No one knew she was here. Picking it up, she brought it inside and put it on the kitchen table. She grabbed a pair of scissors and opened it. There were three flowers in the box wrapped in green tissue paper. Two calla lilies and one red rose. There was also a card. Dread filled her being and she was tempted to throw it out, but she was too curious.

The note said. *Happy Birthday to my one and only*. Only was underlined three times. The flowers were from Billy. How did the bastard know where she was? Chills rocked her as she stared at the flowers. Weren't calla lilies flowers for funerals? The red rose meant love.

She sank into the nearby chair and closed her eyes. It hadn't taken him very long to track her down. Should she tell Colt? No, that would just bring up more questions that she didn't want to answer. Maybe Billy wouldn't dare come to the ranch.

"Who are the flowers from?"

Spring opened her eyes. She wanted to tell him how scared she was. "An old friend. They're for my birthday."

Colt stared at her. He appeared to be waiting for more of an explanation but he wasn't getting one. "Are those white flowers your favorite or something?"

"No, not at all."

He folded his arms in front of him. Doubt was all over his face. "And the rose?"

She gulped hard as her heart raced. "The card wasn't signed. I can't be sure who they are from."

"You know, you just don't want to tell me." His voice grew gruff. "You look scared, but it's your business. If you don't want to tell me so be it." He shook his head, and his mouth formed a straight grim line.

Her eyes shimmered with tears. "I'm afraid, and I can't talk about it now. Give me time, Colt."

Colt studied her as though he was trying to see inside her head. "I'll be back for dinner."

She watched him go out the door, a sob in her throat and tears flowing down her face. He'd acted downright cold toward her. Wave after wave of regret washed over her. Why couldn't she let her guard down for just one minute? The hope she hadn't realized she'd harbored shriveled. She told herself from the beginning Colt was not for her. Men were not for her. It had taken too much for her to realize her mistakes with Billy and she didn't trust herself not to do it again. She hoped she still had his friendship.

The roast was about ready. Pulling it out of the oven, she

realized she had come to think of this place as home in the short time she'd been there. She set the roast on the counter. Colt had a right to know if Billy was going to cause trouble. Thinking about Billy made her ashamed. She should have been stronger, she shouldn't have allowed him to beat her and use her.

Coming to Montana was supposed to be her mulligan, her do-over. Why couldn't the past just be the past? Something bad was bound to happen if Billy showed up.

The door opened, and all three cowboys shuffled in. She pasted a smile on her face. It wasn't their fault she was stupid.

CHAPTER SIX

*C*olt had been walking on eggshells. Spring's face said it all, she was lying and he couldn't figure out why. He could have sworn she was alone in the world but the flowers proved otherwise.

Mailing just three flowers felt deliberate, so he'd looked for some kind of importance. The white flowers he found out were calla lilies. Shady had to clue him in. Once he knew their name, he looked them up on the internet. Some said they were for funerals. The red rose was easy, that meant love. She knew exactly who sent those to her and why. There was her ex-boyfriend out there somewhere. Maybe she still had feelings for him. No, he decided, she seemed scared. The other possibility could be the flowers were some type of warning, but since she hadn't said anything, he couldn't be sure.

He wished he had more experience with women. His dad brought a few home after his mother's death. One smacked Caleb around. Colt lured her out of the house, and then snuck back in locking all the doors. He found it easy enough to be around women, but he never understood them.

His home didn't feel as comfortable these days but he had plenty of work to do to keep him busy. Thank God, he had Holden O'Leary and his brothers helping him out with the horses. Holden was the town's veterinarian. If not for him, Colt wouldn't have been able to help all of the rescues. The amount of medical care they needed was astronomical.

Holden and his brothers were due to come out, and he didn't want any of them to think Spring was fair game. Matthew was old to enough to appreciate a woman like Spring. He planned to stick close to the house today of course. He supposed she was for the taking. He had no claim on her.

Soon enough the sound of trucks driving up toward the house could be heard. Colt met them with a smile.

Spring was already on the front porch, her hand shading her eyes from the sun as she watched the trucks arrive. He liked the way she glanced at him to see if it was all right. He nodded. She started to smile at him then stopped, and he wondered what she was thinking.

He went over to the black pick-up and shook the driver's hand. "Hell, Holden, I've been waiting all day for you to show." Colt chuckled.

Holden cocked his dark-haired head in Spring's direction. "If I had known, I would have dropped by days ago."

Colt didn't like the twinkle in Holden's eyes. "You're married."

Holden gave him a smile of a contented man. "And happily too. There are plenty of bachelors in Carlston searching for a woman as fine as my Summer. How attached are you to this one?" he teased.

Colt could feel his anger start to burn. "She's mine." His heart skipped a beat in shock at his words.

Holden nodded. "You best tell her that."

Colt turned toward the house and swore. Spring was

standing in the middle of the O'Leary brothers. She smiled at them as though they were at some barn dance, and it hit him right in the gut.

"Hey you knuckle heads. We came here to help, not to socialize." Holden walked over to the porch. He grinned. "I can understand the distraction. Ma'am, I'm Holden."

Spring gave him a tentative smile. "Nice to meet you, Holden."

"I'll have my wife stop by and meet you later. She and her gaggle of friends would love to get to know you."

Spring nodded almost hesitantly, and Colt wondered at her reluctance. He'd have thought she'd welcome friends. He knew the other wives, they were nothing but nice.

"Well enough visiting for now, let's get these horses checked out." Colt winked at Spring as she smiled in relief. At least he didn't have to worry she'd fall for one of those O'Learys. It mattered too much to him, and he didn't like it. He had horses to tend to, and no time to moon over a woman.

They walked to the barn, and Holden looked at the newest horse, a bay, and whistled low. "What the hell?" He sighed. "Don't tell me, Cramer?"

"Probably was one of Cramer's but this horse was found wandering about thirty miles west of here." Colt's face hardened. "Think he's going to live?"

Holden swore again. "I don't know." He opened the stall door and slowly went in. "He doesn't shy away."

"He hasn't been skittish at all," Colt told him.

"On the body condition scale I'd give him a one." Holden ran his hands over the gelding gently. "Looks like his belly is bloated, probably full of worms." He gently touched the horse's face next. "His muzzle and jaw are disfigured. Most likely he wasn't getting the right food when he was fed."

Holden patted the horse's neck then let himself out of the stall.

"Colt, I really don't know if this one will make it. It's worth a try though. If ever a horse needed you, it's this one. He's a basket case but I'll treat him. No markings or brand on the horse. It could have come from anywhere."

Colt slapped his Stetson against his thigh. "We both know who the likely culprit is. A basket case, you know that's a good name for him. I'm thankful your brothers came along. There is never enough time in a day to work with each horse."

Holden grinned. "You didn't seem so happy when they were talking to that pretty gal you have up at the house."

Colt felt his face redden. He glanced away. "I have another new one I need you to examine."

Holden kept grinning and walked with Colt passing a few stalls.

Colt nodded toward an appaloosa in his stall. "This one is a sad story. Apparently the barn flooded, so the owner decided to keep the horse in an old horse trailer. He's weak."

Holden nodded. "I can see from here he has rain rot." Holden eased his way into the stall. "This horse had been starved. I can count each rib and look at its spine. Has he been eating?"

"I've had to hand feed him, he's just so weak. He'll eat though. We'll have to treat that fungus he has." Colt hated what had been done to each of the horses that came through.

"Where'd this one come from?"

"The people at the animal shelter wouldn't tell me. It was an owner surrender though. They should have locked those owners up."

"Don't I know it. He'll eventually be fine. Does this one have a name?" Holden fed the horse some straw.

"His name is Thumper." Colt chuckled. "Poor horse, they

named him after a rabbit."

Holden shook his head. "Well, they fed him as though he was a rabbit." He walked out of the stall. "Where are Bibbs and Shady?"

"Someone has to keep track of the cattle. That's what keeps the rescue alive. I've been running on a shoestring."

"How are you holding up? I see the snowmobile is still there."

Colt's heart squeezed painfully. "One day at a time. Spring has helped. She was Caleb's friend from Texas. Poor girl came out here, and she didn't know Caleb passed away. He had offered her a job here, and I almost sent her packing, but I want to honor Caleb's wishes. She's had a hard life, and she can be as skittish as a frightened filly."

Holden laughed. "Well, she came to the right place."

Colt smiled back. "I gave her Heidi's foal. She named him Daybreak."

"Nice," Holden commented. "Guess that means she plans on staying."

Holden's words startled Colt. "I hadn't thought of it that way."

One by one, all of Holden's brother's joined them, Matt, Mark, Luke and John.

John nodded at the rest. "Well that's all of them. We exercised and fed the horses that would let us near them. Did I hear you say Spring likes horses?"

Colt frowned. "Listen guys, Spring's been through the wringer with the last ass she dated. She landed on my porch with more than a few bruises. I'm askin' just let her be."

John smiled. "No problem. If it's healing her soul she needs, then you're the best man for the job."

Holden shook hands with Colt. "I'll be back tomorrow and check on the horses. You take it easy."

Colt watched them leave with envy in his heart. They all

had such camaraderie, the same he had with Caleb. It probably was time to get the smashed snowmobile towed away. It didn't serve any purpose anymore, and it certainly didn't honor Caleb, instead it was a reminder of his one mistake. Colt shook his head and almost laughed. One mistake who was he kidding? They'd gotten into the normal boy trouble together.

Loneliness assailed him. It was something he would live with for some time. There was no escape, just constant reminders. He just hoped that one day he'd be able to remember Caleb with love and laughter instead of as broken and dead.

Staring at the house, he spotted Spring looking out the window at him. She'd tell him the truth when she was ready, wouldn't she? His heart felt heavy, and his breathing came hard. He didn't want to walk on eggshells anymore. He'd give her space. Maybe John was right, she needed to heal. They both did.

He wished he had the right to go inside, grab her up into a big hug and kiss the daylights out of her. He wanted to lay her across his bed, and make sweet love to her but neither was going to happen.

WHAT TO DO? Her nice comfortable living space was no longer comfortable. Colt disliked her. She could see it in his eyes. He stared at her plenty lately, always with a giant frown. At least he wasn't a hitter and not much of a yeller. A frowner wasn't so bad, although it was depressing. Looking out the window, she could see him frowning at her yet again. What to do?

She thought she'd found a place where she could live peacefully, but her peace hadn't lasted. At first, she'd been wary, but then her heart would flutter when he was around. Now this frowning act sat in the pit of her stomach. If only she could lock her emotions away. A frown was just a frown she tried to tell herself.

She set the table. Since she'd been there, both Shady and Bibbs had been constant guests at dinner. It made up for the silences between her and Colt. She knew they could sense something was wrong, but they played along as though nothing was wrong.

The front door opened, and she braced herself. Putting on her best smile, she turned and spied the big frown. "Have you ever heard the saying 'turn that frown upside down'?" He shot her a puzzled look. "You know, it means smile."

Colt hung up his coat. "I might not have gone to college, but I do know what it means." His voice gave away his irritation.

"I just thought maybe you didn't know you've been sporting a perpetual frown for a couple days."

"Oh, you mean since you got those damn flowers and wouldn't tell me who they're from?"

Her smile faded. "Yep, that would be the very frown I mean." She turned from him. It unnerved her that he didn't move, just watched.

"I'm sure Bibbs and Shady will be here any minute." She twisted and untwisted the green kitchen towel she was holding.

"They won't be here for dinner."

"No?"

"I sent them to get rid of the snowmobile." His voice conveyed unbearable pain.

Spring put down the dishtowel and walked over to him. The grief in his eyes pierced her heart, and she wrapped her arms around his waist holding him tight.

He crushed her to him, and there was a lot of need in his

hug. She lightly stroked his back, trying to offer comfort. She heard one sob bubble up out of him, and then all was silent as they held each other.

Colt pulled away and cupped her face. He stroked her cheekbone with the pad of his thumb, and stared into her eyes for the longest time. Dropping his hands, he began to turn away but suddenly he lifted her face with his finger and stared at her lips.

She wet her lips in anticipation and butterflies swarmed in her stomach. He stared into her eyes again and leaned down, but before his lips reached hers, he stepped away.

"We really should eat while it's still hot." She gazed at him. His eyes bespoke of regret, and she wondered if it was regret from not following through with the kiss or regret for thinking about it.

Colt took a step back and ran his fingers through his dark hair. "I'm sorry. I almost, and I shouldn't have."

She turned away and walked to the oven. "Don't worry about it. I know you're grieving, we both are." She pulled the roasted chicken out of the oven and got the potatoes ready to mash. It felt good to exert her pent up pain with each mash. No lumps in her potatoes tonight. A pricking on the back of her neck bothered her. She knew Colt was watching her, and it began to unnerve her.

Finally, she turned around. "Have a seat, dinner is ready."

His curt nod and pain-filled eyes took her appetite away. They sat at the table, but neither one talked. Neither ate very much while tension filled the room, and it was a relief when he finally pushed back from the table, put on his coat and left.

Spring touched her lips and wondered what his kiss would have been like. His regret for even thinking about kissing her, stayed with her. Why did everything have to be so hard? Just for once, she wished she traveled the easy route.

CHAPTER SEVEN

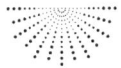

Spring walked out onto the big porch. She could feel it in the warming air, the sense of newness, the sense of spring. It's the season for which she was named. It also brought a lot of disappointment. Every year she told herself this would be the year, the year where new, good things would happen. The new leaves, grass, and flowers all lent to her hope. It was still her favorite. It was a time to dream.

She didn't know what she even wanted to wish for this year. Colt acted stony and guarded. She wasn't even sure he still liked her. Not being liked was something she was used to and normally she didn't care but somehow, she cared now. Colt was a man to be admired. He was honest and gentle. His values surprised her. He believed in the myth if you worked hard, you could make a go of things, and he believed a man's word had value.

Sometimes things weren't that easy. She'd worked hard all her life and she had nothing to show for it. She took a deep breath and negated her last thought. She was here, and no one promised her a romantic, happy ending. As long as they could co-exist, they'd be fine, right?

A truck came up the drive, and Stone McCoy got out with a package in his hands. He smiled at her. "Nice day isn't it?"

Spring returned his smile. "Yes, I was just enjoying it."

"This was delivered to us by mistake. It has your name on it." He walked to the porch and handed it to her.

"Thank you." Her voice sounded chipper but dread filled her. "Won't you come in for a cup of coffee?"

"Wish I had the time. Is Colt in the barn? I need to ask him about a horse."

"Yes, I believe he is. Say hi to Winter and Rachael for me when you get home."

His gray eyes twinkled. "I sure will. Have a good day."

The box wasn't very big, and she clutched it to her chest as she watched Stone walk across the yard. He looked back at her and waved, and Spring quickly waved back. She did not intend to open the box. She knew who sent it but she couldn't just throw it away either. Stone was bound to tell Colt about it.

The box became heavier as she stepped inside the house. By the time she made it to the kitchen table, her heart felt buried under the weight. She placed it in the middle of the table and sat down. Realizing her hands shook, she clasped them together. Why wouldn't Billy leave her alone? It'd been bad enough she had to flee from him. Now he'd found her, she didn't know what to think.

There'd been a time when she adored Billy and the protection he provided her. She watched him manipulate people to get what he wanted. He was so good he actually believed his lies of being a good man and a good provider. At the time, he amazed her. He got whatever he wanted, to hell with consequences or who got hurt. Now she knew better, much better. If only she'd caught on before he'd stolen her soul.

That's what she felt at the end, he'd stolen her soul. Her whole sense of what was right and wrong became warped. He was the very devil, and if it hadn't been for Caleb, Billy would still have a hold on her. Caleb helped her to reject Billy and take her soul back. Now Caleb wasn't even here for her to thank. She could repay him by being more of a friend to Colt.

He came storming through the door. He didn't even glance at her; his gaze was on the unopened package. His brows furrowed and he sighed. "Aren't you going to open it?"

Her gaze met his defiant one. "No."

"Why not? It's probably something from your boyfriend"

"*Ex*-boyfriend."

He studied her face. "Does he know that or is he waiting for you?"

She hesitated and turned from his gaze. "I would think he'd know I wasn't coming back."

"Looks to me like he wants you back." He moved until he could catch her gaze. "If you want to go, don't stay for me. I'm fine."

His words lanced her heart, and she briefly glanced away. Her hands still clasped each other, but her whole body shook. Taking a deep breath, she stood and locked gazes with him. "I know you say I have a choice as to whether I leave or not. Truthfully, leaving wasn't my intent but it seems to be your wish. I never meant to make you mad." She placed a hand on his arm. "Don't worry about it, Colt. It's not the first time I've been asked to leave, and it won't be the last. Someday I will find what I'm searching for and sadly it's not here." Spring gave him a weak smile and let go of him. She glanced away. She couldn't look at him.

"Wait. I'm sorry. I don't want you to go."

Spring turned and was surprised to see his sad smile. The circles under his eyes broke her heart. Compassion for this cowboy overwhelmed her. He was her cowboy. That realization scared her but it also made her heart full.

"Colt, I just can't live like this. This is your home, and you should feel comfortable in it, not dancing around my feelings. Unfortunately, I know when it's time to go."

The sound of his boots on the hardwood floor echoed loudly. He reached for her and drew her against him. His heart beat erratically. All she'd ever wanted in life was suddenly right there, wrapping his comforting arms around her. She closed her eyes, trying to prolong the special feeling. When he let go, all warmth and happiness departed, leaving her bereft. She stepped back, keeping her glance on the floor.

"You're right. I have been avoiding my feelings for you. I've been waiting for the moment when you tell me you're leaving ever since you got here."

"And I've been waiting for you to tell me to go." The silence was awkward, and she didn't know what to say.

Colt smiled. "At least we're on the same page. The wrong page but the same." He reached out and tucked a strand of her hair behind her ear. "Why didn't you open it?"

Her gaze shot up and met Colt's. "I already know who it's from, and I don't want it."

His sigh of relief was evident. He ran his fingers through his thick dark hair. "Is it from your ex?"

Spring nodded. "Yes it's from Billy."

"You're afraid of him. He's the one who left bruises."

"Yes." Her face grew warm with shame.

"Why is he sending you packages? Do you plan to go back to him?"

"No, never." She walked to the door, grabbed her coat and kept walking.

She continued toward the barn. Did Colt really think

she'd go back to Billy? She had to admit there was a time she would have talked herself into going back, but now she never wanted to set eyes on him again. She'd changed since she left him. She did have self-worth, and she could make it in the world without him.

———

COLT WAS AT A LOSS. The pieces had all been there in front of him. Why did he let his ego get in the way? She'd probably been afraid since the flowers arrived, and he was just a jealous fool. Hell, he didn't know enough about women, he just saw the flowers and he jumped to conclusions. Maybe he needed to handle her the same way he handled his horses. He could see the fear in her eyes. Why was it so hard for him?

He'd have to figure out a way to make her tell him what was really going on. The fear in her eyes got to him. Grabbing his coat, he headed for the barn. He walked inside and was treated to a spectacular sight. Spring was kneeling down in front of the pen Heidi and Daybreak were in, murmuring something to them, and Daybreak acted as though she entranced him. He hung on every word as though he could understand what she was saying, and maybe he did. Nothing surprised him about horses anymore.

"You look like a natural with horses." Colt walked closer to her.

She jumped, and her head whipped around to look at him. "I didn't hear you come in." Her voice was cold enough to leave a chill.

"I'm sorry. You have a right to your privacy. I'm as bad as the town busybodies, needing to know everything."

Spring gazed at him as though she was trying to decide if he was sincere. "Isn't he beautiful?"

He nodded. "Beautiful would be the right word." He stared at her.

She must have noticed his meaning because she blushed and looked away. "I suppose I should go on into the house. I have laundry to do." She stood up but as she passed Colt, he grabbed her hand and held it until she met his gaze.

"The laundry can wait. You're not here to be the house cleaner, and I will show you how to do the bookkeeping so you're not just cooking and cleaning all the time. I'm sorry for being a jerk about the package. I don't even know why it bothers me so much. I don't want you to leave, and you can have as many packages arrive, as you want. I acted like an overbearing boyfriend."

She nodded smiling tightly, and he couldn't tell what she was thinking. Maybe that was for the best.

"We could be friends though." He waited for a real smile but it never came.

"Colt, we're really just employee and employer. Simple is best."

He watched her walk away. Damn, simple wasn't exactly what he wanted, or was it? He removed his Stetson and slapped it against his thigh. Hell, he didn't know what he wanted. His Dad had been right, women make you plain crazy.

His cell phone rang. As he answered, he started to run toward the house. There was a horse in trouble, and he was needed.

"I need to run, darlin'. Don't wait on me for dinner."

She turned toward him. "What happened?"

"There's a horse, and I'm hoping it's only one that was bought by old man Sweeny. He buys them at auction and from rescue places then he sells them across the border for more money. He's supposed to be on the banned list but somehow he slips under the radar. I need to hurry before he gets rid of the horse or horses." He grabbed his gloves and kissed her on the cheek. Her eyes widened. The kiss surprised him as much as it surprised her.

SPRING WAITED all day for Colt to come home. A smile graced her lips; she really considered this place her home. However, a frown quickly replaced it as she reminded herself it wasn't wise to get comfortable in one place. Lessons so hard learned should be remembered. Still, she had her gaze on the front window.

She saw some of the horses in the barn the other day, and the sight of a few of them broke her heart. How could people not feed a horse? A few looked like skeletons. Colt told her sometimes the owners would move and leave the horses to fend for themselves. He had a good heart, and the horses sensed it. Colt's truck and horse trailer along with two others pulled up to the barn. She grabbed her coat and hurried outside. She was almost at the trailer when Colt blocked her way. His shoulders were so wide she couldn't see behind him.

"Colt, is something wrong?" Her brows furrowed.

"I wish to God I could say no, Spring. I don't want you to see the horses just yet."

"But, why?"

"Honey, that bastard tried to remove any ID on the horses." The bleakness of his expression tore at her.

"What does that mean?"

"Some were branded and one tattooed. I can't go into it now. There were six horses in all. Holden is right behind me. I need you to go inside, please."

She nodded and gave him a compassionate smile. "Of course. I'll be there when you need me." Reaching out she patted his arm, their gazes locked and held before she walked back toward the house. He was a good man, his actions proved it. If only she'd come from a different background and had never been mixed up with Billy...

Opening the front door, she shook her head. What was she thinking? He was grieving and needed a friend, nothing more, and she'd best remember that before her heart became entrenched.

She took off her jacket and boots and turned. The first thing she saw was the package from Billy, sitting there bigger than life on the kitchen table. No matter how hard she tried to look away from it, she couldn't. The thought of opening it paralyzed her but she wasn't one to back down.

Taking a deep breath, she marched over to the table and ripped the box open. Horrified, she covered her mouth with her hand to keep the screams in. The implication of the ring inside was not lost on her. Her legs gave way, and she grabbed the back of the wooden chair, easing herself down into it, her gaze fixed on the ring, her ring. It was too much, and tears flowed down her face.

So many things happened in the foster homes, horrible things but the worst for her was when a girl named Teresa went missing. Not that she'd had any type of love for the bully. Teresa stole the ring right off her hand and backhanded her after. It was right around the time she'd met Billy at her last home. She kept her mouth shut, that's just the way things were. Billy had always been violent but not to her, not at first. Her hands shook, her heart clenched in denial and it became too hard to breathe but she knew the truth. Billy got the ring back, and Teresa was gone. A chill ran up her spine. She'd have to tell Colt, he deserved to know she put him in danger. There wasn't a doubt in her mind Billy would hurt Colt to get her back.

Exhaustion filled her, and she couldn't take much more.

Caleb's death was still a lance of pain in her mind and now this threat of Billy knowing where she was. The weight of the world fell upon her, and she prayed she wouldn't be crushed. Tears filled her eyes, and she swiped at them with the back of her hand to no avail; there were too many. Reaching into the box, she took the ring and fisted it in her hand. It was her only possession from her mother, and even though the woman had done nothing to help her in her entire life, she still treasured it. It turned her finger green but the value to her was priceless. It gave her a sense of connection.

It wasn't worth getting back, however Billy did it. Spring hiccupped. Teresa was never seen again, and it wouldn't be a big stretch of her imagination to believe Billy had something to do with her disappearance.

The door opened and closed behind her. What to tell Colt? He needed to know, and she hoped he wouldn't think less of her for being mixed up with a man like Billy.

Colt stared at her for a moment and then sat down next to her. He seemed to be at a loss for words. He took her hand and sat quietly next to her as though he understood her need to gather her thoughts.

"I opened the package." Her voice was barely audible.

Colt glanced at the empty box. "Anything you want to talk about?"

Spring nodded, got up grabbed a tissue and mopped up her face. She sat back down and put the ring on the table. "This was inside."

"I see." He frowned as he took the ring, examined it and put it back down. "It's from—"

"Billy, it's from Billy. It belongs to me, but a girl at the last home I was at stole it, and I never thought I'd see it again." Colt's chocolate eyes held too much compassion, and she had to turn her head and look at the wall.

"The girl who took it from me, her name was Teresa and soon after she stole my ring she went missing. I never gave it much thought because everyone said she ran away. Now I'm not so sure that's what happened. If Billy had gotten it back from her, why not just give it to me? I'm afraid I've brought Billy to your door, and I thought I knew what he was capable of, but this puts a completely added dimension to his monstrous behavior. He may have killed her, at least that's my fear and it's a message to me. I think he plans to hurt me."

Colt took her hand in both of his large warm ones, then he reached out and wiped away a tear from her cheek with his thumb. "Nobody messes with me and mine. Don't worry, darlin, we'll get it figured out. I know he abused you, but do you think he's capable of murder? It's a big jump from hurting to killing."

"I just don't know. He always protected me at the foster home but once we started living together, he became mean. He wanted to know where I was at all times, and he made me feel as though I couldn't do anything right. He wanted the house kept a certain way, his clothes folded just right and meals cooked to his specifications. I tried so hard to make him happy, convinced that it would get better if I just did things right."

Sighing, he let go of her hand and tucked a stray lock of hair behind her ear. "Why didn't you just leave?"

"And go where?" The bitterness in her voice echoed through the kitchen. Her frustration grew, and she wanted to run and hide. It wasn't her fault, was it? She'd tried so hard to placate Billy but to no avail.

"I'm glad Caleb sent you here. I have a few errands to run, but Bibbs and Shady are working close to the house today. I'll give them a heads up about this creep."

"Thank you." She leaned over, kissed his cheek and pulled away.

Colt gave her a crooked smile. "What does this jerk look like?"

"Blond hair, brown eyes, he's a big guy but not muscular."

"I'll let the others know." He nodded, grabbed his hat and coat and gave her a long look before he went out the door.

She hadn't realized how tense she was until her body began to relax. There was no way she could fight Billy on her own but she didn't want Colt to get hurt. Maybe he was right; it was a big jump from smacking a woman around to killing. Billy must have wrestled the ring from Teresa before she left. Maybe, just maybe, it wasn't a threat. What if a gift was just a gift? Spring shook her head nothing was simple with Billy.

COLT WENT TO TOWN, talked to the sheriff, and was surprised the old man acted as if he wanted to help. He actually said he'd keep an eye out.

The turn off to Summer and Holden's place lay just ahead. Colt gunned the engine and headed to their house. Today there was a meeting with Holden, Jonas and Stone. It was good to have friends even if he hadn't wanted to talk to them recently. He'd still be in his own world of bitterness if it wasn't for Spring's intervention.

The familiar two-story house came into view, and Holden stepped out onto the massive porch to meet him. Colt got out of the truck and greeted Holden with a handshake. "Thanks for having the meeting here. I don't want Spring to worry."

"No problem, come on in. Stone and Jonas are inside."

Colt followed his friend into the house and was immediately greeted by Holden's wife, Summer. Her honey blonde hair was as bright as her smile, and her blue eyes were filled with worry. She reached out and hugged him. "You okay, cowboy?"

Colt nodded. "Doing okay."

Summer nodded and let go.

Colt glanced over toward the kitchen. "Good Lord, what have you been feeding them? They are growing like weeds."

Holden's brothers, Matt, Mark, Luke and John all nodded to him. "Summer's a good cook," Luke stated as he popped another cookie in his mouth. They all resemble each other, dark hair and eyes. Holden had been raising them since their mother died.

However, it didn't matter how many cookies they ate, they'd never be as big as his friend Jonas. That man stood well over six feet and had shoulders that filled a doorway. Colt nodded at him too. "Thanks for coming."

"Glad to help."

Stone stood up from the couch, a bit wary of approaching Colt. "We good?"

Colt nodded. "We're good."

Holden gestured for them to sit in the family room. "Tell me what's going on."

Colt cleared his throat. "You probably know I have a little gal staying at my place. She is, was a friend of Caleb's. I got into rescuing horses because of Caleb. He was always bringing home mistreated animals and expecting me to fix them. Well, anyway he sent Spring to me in the same vein. Her boyfriend was mistreating her so Caleb gave her a ticket to Montana."

"I heard you had a woman over there," Jonas said.

"I know I got you all into the horse rescue cause, and I've admired each of you for your contribution of time and money to help these animals. Now, I'm here to ask for help for Spring. I'm not sure we need help, but her old boyfriend has been sending odd presents and frankly I can see in her eyes she's beyond scared."

"What can we do to help?" Stone asked.

"I just need some extra eyes and ears. Carlston is a small enough town that strangers stand out. I'd like a heads up if anyone sees him."

"No problem. Just how dangerous do you think he is?" Holden asked glancing at his brothers who were listening with rapt attention.

"He beat her pretty badly before she left. He knows she's at my place. He sent her flowers and a ring—"

"Maybe he's courting her," John, the youngest brother, yelled from the kitchen.

"The flowers were a strange combo. There was a red rose and some calla lilies. It seemed strange and it startled Spring. The ring was a ring she once owned, and some girl who is missing took it from her. It could be nothing but—"

Jonas stood up. "If you're worried, we're worried. What does this guy look like?"

"Blond hair, brown eyes. She said he's a big fella but not muscular." Colt rubbed the back of his neck.

"So he's a big lug," Summer commented.

Colt smiled; leave it to Summer to break the tension. "A lug he is."

"So, let me get this straight he sent funeral flowers and a ring a missing girl had? How'd he end up with the ring?" Stone leaned forward.

"It's all speculation. Billy might not know what the flowers meant, and he could have gotten the ring back from the girl before she took off. The fact Spring is scared is good enough for me. Like I said I'd just like a heads up if anyone sees him." Colt stood up, stretching his long legs.

Jonas patted him on his back. "Don't you worry, we have

your back. So, tell us about Spring. Stone here says she's a sweet girl. Is she as pretty as he says?"

He felt his face grow hot. "She's like a pretty filly that shies away. She came here without a coat or boots and when I bought her some, she practically cried. She says she grew up in the foster home system and never had much."

The men nodded.

"A pretty filly?" Summer rolled her eyes. "Must you all equate women with horses?"

Colt laughed. "It's the only language I know, darlin'"

"Tell her I'll be out to visit. I want to make sure she has everything a woman needs. A woman, not a horse," she said pointedly.

Colt kissed her cheek. "You do that. I think she'd like a visit from you."

Holden stood and shook Colt's hand. "We got this. We'll be on the lookout for the lug. You take care of that little filly." He grunted as Summer punched him in the shoulder.

Colt winked at Summer. "Thank you, all of you."

Colt walked out into the sunshine, the warmth on his face was life affirming. *Caleb you did the right thing by sending Spring here.*

Driving home, he felt better than he had in days. His heart still wrenched every time he thought of Caleb, but he knew now he had good friends.

He drove up to his ranch and was surprised just how quiet it was. *Damn.* He hurried from his truck to the house and opened the door. Bibbs, Shady and Spring all sat at the kitchen table playing cards.

His gaze fell upon hers and locked. He could see the beginning of trust in her eyes. They were on the right road, he was certain of it. What road, he didn't know just yet.

"I said to stay close to the house, not sit inside and play cards."

Bibbs and Shady both shot him guilty looks. "Just taking a break, Boss," Shady mumbled.

They quickly stood up, and Bibbs muttered another apology.

"Sit, we've worked hard this week. What are we playing?"

CHAPTER EIGHT

Spring grew increasingly upset as she watched Shady lean against the barn staring at the house. It had been two weeks since she opened the package, and she'd been under constant surveillance. Usually it was Shady, but the other two took turns too. When Colt stood watch, she felt like a bug under a magnifying glass.

She protested a couple times, but Colt was adamant. Heck with Colt, she'd had enough, but what could she do about it? She had nowhere else to go, and she didn't want to take a chance of Colt getting angry. He was looking out for her but she had to have some alone, unwatched time.

Relying on Billy got her in this situation, if it even was really a situation. No other packages had appeared, and there had been no sign of him. Maybe it was time to let the whole thing go and get on with her life.

She grabbed a sweater and went out the door. A walk would clear her head, and she wanted to see the crocuses up close. Other flowers were sprouting up a little ways from the house; it was spring, and the weather was finally getting warmer.

Stealthily she crept out the backdoor, giving Shady the slip. She wouldn't be gone long and, he probably wouldn't even notice.

The wind had a tinge of coolness to it, reminding her winter hadn't been long ago. A lot of the ranch was muddy from the melted snow, and it was near impossible to keep the floors in the house clean. The mud sucked at one foot, then the other as she walked along the back trail.

The buds on the trees promised a beautiful summer. The world looked new. That's what she loved about spring; it always was a chance for a new start. Maybe this year she'd actually be able to say her life had changed for the better.

The lilac, white and yellow crocuses were even prettier up close, and she couldn't help the huge grin that graced her face. She hoped some of the other flowers beginning to sprout were daffodils, her favorite. The air smelled fresh and clean, and she closed her eyes turning her head to the sun, feeling comfort from the warm glow.

A twig snapped from behind, and she opened her eyes and turned. Her perfect moment ended with Colt's scowl. He was a gentle soul, but she couldn't help the fear that was inside her every time he was mad.

She gave him a tentative smile. "Hi."

"What are you doing out here? You scared me half to death! I have better things to do than look for you while you're looking at flowers." His frown deepened, and her heart dropped.

It hurt knowing she was merely an inconvenience. Somehow, she thought their friendship was on solid ground. "Sorry." She tried to walk around him back to the house, but he gently grabbed her arm.

"I would have taken you if you wanted to see them." His brown eyes glittered, and his voice was gruff.

"I know." She pulled away and started walking. How was

it possible to feel such joy one minute and sorrow the next? Her shoulders slumped. Grateful is how she should be instead of annoyed but it was hard to remember.

"Hey wait!" Colt ran until he was beside her. "I didn't mean to be an ass. I've gotten so used to watching out for you. I couldn't stand to lose you too."

Spring stopped, her mouth formed an O while she stared at him. "Then it's me who should apologize. I never looked at it from your point of view. I mean I know you've been getting less work done with me here, and since you don't have the extra time to teach me the bookkeeping right now, I was thinking about going into town to look for a job..."

Colt turned her toward him, stared into her eyes, and she could see all the anguish he carried. He leaned toward her as he turned his stare to her lips. Her heart beat faster in antici-pation, and she leaned forward.

"Oh, hell, I'm sorry." Colt turned away and began to walk to the house leaving her puzzled and sad.

It would have just made things awkward between them. She really didn't want him to kiss her, though a test run would have been nice.

COLT STRODE INTO THE BARN, went straight to the tack room and closed the door. What kind of man takes advantage of a sweet girl like Spring?

Really, who does that? Knowing what she's gone through. He sat in his work chair and banged his fist against the wooden table. This was plain crazy, and he needed to get a grip on his emotions before he scared her off.

Finding her gone had put him in full panic mode, and he hadn't meant to wipe the joy off her face. She'd looked like a fairy nymph standing there among the flowers with her head tilted toward the sun, and he ruined her moment of happiness. It was official: he was a jerk. He knew better than to approach a filly that way.

Maybe Summer is right, you can't equate women with horses. In the past he just smiled at women and called them darlin' yet he never really had a serious relationship.

It had been a couple weeks, and Billy hadn't shown his face in Carlston. Maybe it was time to loosen the reins. Damn, now he'd gone and equated Spring with a horse again. This was going to take some practice.

"Boss?" Bibbs knocked on the door.

"Come in."

Bibbs appeared in the open door, his face flushed and shuffling his feet back and forth.

Colt's eyes narrowed. "What's wrong? Did you two get thrown off your horses again?"

"No, nothing like that. You see, Spring asked me to drive her into town to find a job. I had to say no."

"You did the right thing."

Bibbs held his hat in his hands, running his fingers along the brim in a circle. "Glad you agree because there will be no dinner tonight and tomorrow is debatable."

Colt laughed, a deep rumbling laugh, and Bibbs visibly relaxed. "Well, don't that beat all? I'll talk to her, but I can't guarantee she'll cook. I'll make us something if worse comes to worst." Colt laughed again. "She really said that? She's got spunk."

Bibbs smiled. "She sure does. You going in to talk to her?"

"Hell no, I'm going to wait until she cools down."

"Good choice, Boss."

An hour later, he felt as though he was on an even enough keel to talk to Spring. Crying women he could hold, riled women, he didn't have a clue. Now if she was a horse... He smiled. He needed to remember women were not horses.

Walking into the house, he found Spring sitting on the couch, with her feet up, watching TV. She hadn't really watched much TV the whole time she'd been there. She glanced at him with blazing, blue eyes. He gave her his most cocky smile, confident she'd smile back. It didn't happen; instead, she looked back at the TV.

He frowned. "Hi, how's it going?"

There was no response at all, and he began to doubt himself. Maybe a riled woman was better than a silent one. "Listen if you are waiting for an apology for not allowing you to go into town, I'm not going to give you one. I think Billy might not be such a threat, but until we talk about it, you and I, I don't feel comfortable with you leaving the ranch."

Her chin lifted and her eyes widened. He had her full attention. "Allow? You didn't just say that did you? I'm not your problem, I'm not your property, so where do you get off allowing me to do anything? And you can stop smiling at me!"

"If you live under my roof—"

Her mouth hung open. "Fine, I'm sure I can find another roof. I'm not without skills you know. I'm not some little waif you took in. I'm a woman with her own mind, and I refuse to allow anyone to tell me what to do again!"

Maybe a silent woman was better after all. Her hands clenched and unclenched as her mouth formed a taut line. There was fear in her eyes. He would bet she hadn't yelled at anyone in sometime. Perhaps he could gentle her. "Damn."

"Damn what? Damn me, Damn you?"

"No I promised my friend Summer I'd stop thinking of women as horses. I saw her the other day."

Spring's eyes narrowed as she flipped her long red hair behind her shoulder. "Good, you can have Summer cook your meals from now on. I'm leaving in the morning. It took every ounce of courage I had to leave Billy, and I refuse to live with a controlling man again."

"I'm not—"

"Oh, yes you are." She stood, walked to her room, promptly slammed the door and the lock clicked.

How did he get to be the bad guy? Everyone said he was easygoing, fun to be around, dependable. He sighed. He was all those things before Caleb died. His heart twisted once more at the thought of his brother, pain still as sharp as the day of the accident.

He went to the refrigerator and took out everything he needed to make sandwiches. Maybe she would change her mind in the morning.

Who was he kidding? She wanted to be as far away from him as she could.

SPRING WAS NEVER SO happy to see the sunrise. She dozed on and off all night, listening to the sounds of the house. The argument with Colt shook her hard. She couldn't believe she blasted him like that. The need to stand firm outgrew her fear. Being on her own was best for all involved.

She'd just wait until Shady arrived. He'd give her a ride or she'd walk. Either way she intended to leave. She had no malice toward Colt, but she couldn't take the risk after his outburst yesterday. She knew all about men and how they changed from nice to wicked. She just couldn't take that chance after finally getting away from it.

Grabbing her suitcase, she walked out of her room and out of the house. Shady's truck had just pulled up. She went and talked to him for a minute, and shortly after, she was on her way to Carlston. It felt wrong not to say goodbye to Colt, but it couldn't be helped.

Carlston was a small town but it had a few diners and restaurants where she hoped to find a job. If anything, she was a damn good waitress. As far as where to live, she prayed an answer would come to her. If not, it wouldn't be the first time she'd had to sleep in the street.

Shady hardly said a word the whole drive to town. He let her off in front of Lucy's Deli, tipped his hat and drove off. Loneliness washed over her, but she was here to find work, not to feel sorry for herself.

Lucy's looked like a likely enough place to start.

Three hours later, she sat on a park bench in front of the community center, wired from too much coffee. Everyone had been nice but no one was hiring. A few businesses didn't open until afternoon so there was still hope.

Sighing, she watched the townspeople go about their day, visiting the general store or stopping into Rex's Barbershop. In fact, it looked as though Rex's was a town hot spot. At least the weather was nice.

A woman with neon green hair and matching nails walked by, stopped and came back her way. "New in town?"

Spring nodded. "Looking for a job."

The woman sat down next to her. "I'm Mindy Sue, I work part-time at the veterinarian's office while I go to school."

"I'm Spring, it's nice to meet you."

"Colt's friend? Where are you staying, if you don't mind my asking?"

"Yes, I know Colt. And I guess I'll figure out where to stay after I find a job."

Mindy Sue smiled. "Come with me, I'll make a few calls and see about a job. A place to live, I'm not sure about, maybe Holden will know."

"Holden? You work for Holden?"

Mindy Sue cocked her head to one side. "Sure do, he's the best vet around."

"I met him briefly. He's a friend of Colt's."

"Come with me. Colt wouldn't take kindly if I left you out here you being his woman and all."

Stunned, Spring stared at Mindy Sue. "His woman?"

"There I go putting my foot in my mouth again I didn't mean anything by it. Come on the least I can do is get you a cup of coffee."

Spring nodded tentatively. It was the only offer she'd had all day. She could do without more coffee but she accepted.

The animal clinic was small and inviting. Holden must be a busy man considering all the horses she'd seen at Colt's that needed medical attention. "I really don't want you to go to any trouble. If you could just give me a few leads about jobs, I'll be out of your hair." She quickly glanced away. Why did she mention hair?

"I change my hair color at least once a week, you'll get used to it. I'll need to make a few calls. I like to think I have my finger on the pulse of this town, but it's not true. I can't keep up with it all. What type of work are you looking for?"

"Waitressing is what I do best, although Colt was going to teach me how to do the bookkeeping for the ranch. I already applied at Lucy's Deli, Carlston Diner, Frank's Place."

"Here," Mindy Sue said as she handed her a cup of coffee. "Take a seat this might take a while."

"Really I can do it—"

"Do what?" Spring turned her head and realized Holden had come into the clinic. His dark hair and eyes gave him a dreamy type of look.

"Hey, Holden. Spring needs a job, and I was going to call around to see what's available."

His gaze pinned Spring to her chair. "Why aren't you at Colt's? Did something happen?"

"No, no, I just thought it might be better if I did things for myself." Her face heated.

"Smothering you was he?"

"No, I just wanted a change."

Holden leaned against Mindy Sue's desk and crossed his arms in front of him. "Colt sent you away?"

"No."

"I have to tell you he's one of the most upstanding guys I know, and Summer loves him to pieces."

A chill went through her. "Summer? He did mention his girlfriend. I haven't met her yet."

Holden grinned. "Damn, I hope that rumor isn't true. Summer is my wife."

Spring closed her eyes and shook her head. Nothing made sense anymore. She opened them. "Your wife?" She put her coffee on the table next to her chair and groaned as she rubbed the back of her neck.

Holden still grinned. "So, you are here because of Summer?"

"She was just the kicker. I went for a walk, Colt went ballistic telling me what I'm not allowed to do, and no man is going to tell me what to do again. I've lived that life and…" Tears threatened to spill.

Mindy Sue sat silently looking from one to the other. She grabbed a tissue from her desk and handed it to Spring.

"Thank you, Mindy Sue."

Holden sat in the chair next to hers. "He didn't want you leaving the ranch did he?"

Spring nodded as she wiped her tears.

"Honey, I know you've been through a lot but so has Colt. He's trying to protect you. I think he feels as though he couldn't save Caleb, so he's trying to save you."

"It never crossed my mind."

"That's because you're too close to the situation," Mindy Sue chimed in.

Spring nodded slowly. "It's done now." She stood up,

grabbed her bag and headed for the door. "Thank you both, but I have a job to find." Turning toward the door, her heart stopped. Colt stood in the doorway, his dark hair tousled as though he'd run his fingers through it a million times and his brown eyes held a kindness that went to her heart.

"I don't suppose you'd like a job at my ranch? I admit the ranch owner can be grouchy and overbearing but he has a few good points too."

She tilted her head. "Oh? Like what?"

Colt cleared his throat, and he gripped his Stetson. "He is kind to animals and he's not a slob."

She smiled. "It that your recommendation? There must be more."

"He's sorry as all get out, and most of all he misses you. Oh and Heidi and Daybreak have been so sad without you." He winked at her.

"Using those poor animals as enticements? For shame," she teased.

"Is it working?"

Holden stood up, put his hand on the small of her back and gave her a gentle push. "Go on you two. Mindy Sue and I have work to do. Oh and, Spring? I'll bring Summer around to visit soon."

She turned and gazed at Holden. "She's not allowed out without you?"

Holden laughed. "If you only knew. I'm lucky if she allows me."

Spring turned and followed Colt outside. "How did you know where I was?"

"I hightailed it to town when I realized you left and then Mindy Sue called. She saw you sitting on a bench. I guess your suitcase tipped her off to trouble at home."

Heavy Duty always enjoyed being brushed down. It'd been two days since Spring returned. Colt shook his head. "You know boy, there is no figuring the mind of a female."

Heavy Duty snorted. Even the horse knew what he meant. He didn't know how to act in his own house anymore. If he tiptoed, she frowned, if he was polite, she frowned, if he said something nice, she really frowned. "First, she leaves because I'm too controlling and now she hates that I'm nice. You know if it was any other female, I'd just call it a day. Never found one I wanted to go the extra mile for. I'm not saying I love her or anything, Heavy Duty, I don't think I have those feelings inside me. I just like having her around is all."

"Talking to yourself, Boss?" Bibbs asked as he entered the barn.

"Guilty."

"Well, Spring is not happy with you. Something about you not leaving your socks on the floor anymore. I don't understand women."

Colt's laugh started low in his chest and rumbled out deeply. "Me neither, Bibbs. I can't seem to win. If I'm too nice she's in a snit, if I'm quiet she frowns, and I'm not sure what she wants. I even offered to take her to Autumn's restaurant for dinner, and you would have thought I'd committed a crime. Now the whole sock thing has me thinking she's a bit touched in the head."

Bibbs laughed, then his eyes widened, and he abruptly stopped laughing. Colt turned around, and there stood Spring with her hands on her hips, glaring at him.

"See you later, Boss," Bibbs said as he skedaddled.

"I'd ask if you were here to see me but I know better. Both Heidi and Daybreak would probably like a visit from you." He went back to grooming his horse. It was so quiet he glanced in her direction and there she still stood in the doorway. "Was there something you needed?"

"You are infuriating, do you know that, Colt O'Malley? If I was a person of violence I'd crack you in the head with a skillet or something."

His brow furrowed. "I've been doing everything I can to be nice and not upset you."

"I know, and that's the problem, you've been too stinking nice. I'm not a flower that will wilt. I come from a tough background, and I know a snow job when I see it. Just cut it out."

"Too stinking nice?" He threw back his head and laughed. "Hell, I thought you left because I was mean."

She kept her gaze on the ground and shuffled her feet back and forth before answering. "I like you for you. I don't like the mean Colt but I don't like the sugary sweet, everything is fine, Colt either."

"I guess I don't know what you want." He led Heavy Duty to his stall and closed the door behind the horse. "Maybe you could explain it to me?"

"I mean I want you to be happy, but I know you're not. You're still grieving, and I don't want you to be anything you're not around me."

He walked toward her until they were standing toe to toe. She tilted her head to look at his face. "You're lovely did you know that?"

Her blue eyes widened in surprise, and she shook her head. "No." The blush across her face made him grin.

"Well, you are." He leaned down and gave her a quick peck on her rosy lips.

She turned her face from him. "I...this was nice, I think..." She ducked her head, pulled away and headed for the door. Once there she stopped, turned back and stared at him. "Maybe we can do that again sometime." Her face grew bright red.

Colt nodded and watched as she flew out the door and ran to the house. Heavy Duty snorted. "You are so right, women are not meant to be understood. What is this 'be myself' stuff? I'm always myself, aren't I? I mean I'm me, so who else am I? Damn, Heavy Duty, now I'm some sort of philosopher. Caleb was always the smart one."

I wish you were here Caleb. The pain in his heart grew, instead of getting better, it was worse. Time was supposed to make it better but whoever said that was a liar. He had moments where he could forget the pain, but there was so much that reminded him of his brother that it all came creeping back often.

He walked over to Buckskin's stall. Buckskin was Caleb's horse. Colt smiled sadly remembering their disagreement on the horse's name. Caleb thought since the horse was buckskin his name should be Buckskin. Colt told him that was no name for a horse, and Caleb smiled at him with that cocky grin of his and told him that Colt wasn't a good name for a human.

He sighed as he patted Buckskin's neck. The horse whinnied. "I know I miss him too." Perhaps the grief would never leave him, he didn't know.

Shady walked in wiping his sweaty forehead with his shirtsleeve. "It's starting to get a bit warm out there. Hey, any idea what's for dinner?"

"No idea. I'm just glad Spring is cooking again."

"She sure is changeable don't you think?" Shady asked.

"Changeable?"

"Yeah, you know, moody. One minute she can't stand you, then she likes you, then she's mad at you again. If you want my advice I'd leave my socks on the floor if it makes her happy."

Colt shook his head. "I might take your advice. She told me to be myself. She doesn't like the nice me, she doesn't like the ordering her around me. I don't know what she wants."

"Just treat her like you treat us."

Colt cocked his head to one side. "How do I treat you?"

"You tell us what to do but that's because we work for you, but so does she. Mostly we kid around with each other, we have each other's back, and we don't tiptoe around each other in fear of hurting feelings. Treat her like one of the guys, which will probably make her happy."

"When did you get to be so smart?"

Shady smiled. "I've always been smart but my mama told me to never act smarter than my boss."

Colt chuckled. "Your mama was a very wise woman." He slapped Shady on the back as he passed him. He stepped outside, took a deep breath and shrugged his shoulders. Shady actually made sense for a change, go figure.

SPRING'S HANDS wouldn't stop shaking. She'd been kissed before, but she never cared for it much. She touched her lips and smiled. Colt made her feel special somehow. It was a brief little kiss but still—

The door opened, and she felt her face heat when Colt walked inside. She put on her best smile for him, but he didn't smile back. He glanced at her, giving her a brief nod, and without a word, he went to his room.

Crestfallen, she stared at the closed door and swallowed hard. Did he regret kissing her? Once a fool always a fool, she should have known better than to start weaving dreams together. The pain of rejection stung, and she wished she knew what was going on. He was the one who kissed her, but she was the one to stop. A sudden coldness settled over her, rejection was the one thing she knew all about. Her whole life had been one rejection after another, but she had to buck up. She had to be made of sterner stuff.

Colt's ranch seemed different to her but the world was the same no matter where you went, and she didn't have the power to change it. Sighing, she went back to cooking dinner. She was fortunate to have a job and a place to lay her head. No one ever claimed she'd have love or romance. Colt couldn't be blamed for not being attracted to her. Billy had told her often enough that she wasn't anything special. Yet for a moment in the barn, she had been special.

What would Caleb have thought of the whole situation? Peacefulness came to her. He would have been happy she was finally done lying to herself about Billy and keeping company with Colt. His easy laughter was missed, as was his gentle, caring nature. No more running away like a spoiled child, she would work for a roof over her head and be grateful.

Dinner was finally ready, and Spring was doubly happy Bibbs and Shady ate with them. They carried the whole conversation. Colt seemed lost in thought, and he was adept at avoiding her probing stare. Her heart squeezed the whole time but she sat straight and tall with her shoulders back. There was no way she was going to show her feelings now. It wouldn't change anything.

Bibbs and Shady both escaped as soon as the meal was done. In fact, they practically ran out of the house, and she couldn't blame them. The tension in the air was thick.

Colt stood and picked up his coffee mug. "I'm going to hit the hay, goodnight." He walked away without looking at her. Right before he went into his room, he turned. "I'll leave my socks on the floor for you."

CHAPTER NINE

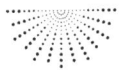

$\mathcal{S}$itting on the front porch a few days later, Spring grinned as she sipped her coffee. No more guard dogs, but she had a feeling they were still keeping an eye on her from somewhere, which was fine. There was still tension between her and Colt, but it was easing. He didn't look at her much anymore, and it stung, but he was more like his old self and best of all, he treated her like a normal person, not like a baby bird who had yet to fly.

There might not be long glances between them, but she still looked her full. Colt was a fine specimen of maleness. She'd laughed when he referred to Billy as The Lug. In comparison, that was a good name for him. Colt was all muscle, and the slightest things were making her stomach flutter. If he rolled up his sleeves and exposed the dark hair on his strong arms, the fluttering started, and she had no control over it. If he hadn't shaved, if his hair was wet, if he bent over... She had to stop thinking about him.

Hyperawareness, that's what it was and surely it would fade eventually. She shook her head, sooner would be better.

As promised, he left his socks on the floor. He understood what she'd been trying to say about being himself.

"Lost in thought?" Colt took her by surprise.

Her face warmed, and she glanced at him briefly. "Something like that." She pretended to find her coffee fascinating, averting her gaze.

"How about going into town for dinner tonight?"

"I can make us something."

"Spring, look at me. You didn't come all the way to Montana to be my housekeeper. I've been meaning to get you started on the books and I will. Let's just take a break for once. It's fine, it'll just be two friends eating dinner, besides I owe Autumn a visit, and I feel bad I haven't been to see her. Come with me?" He cocked his right eyebrow and gave her one of his big grins.

She looked up and couldn't help but smile back. "Autumn?"

"Jonas' wife, she owns a restaurant in town. I have to warn you it's a vegetarian place without a steak in sight. Surprisingly, the food is still good."

"A vegetarian restaurant in cattle country? That's brave. I'd be happy to meet her."

"Great it's a date. I mean, not a date but it'll be fun, and I think you'll like her."

The smile on her face threatened to wither but she brazened it out. "It'll be nice, thank you."

"Good, see ya later."

She couldn't resist staring at his sexy rear end as he walked away. She needed to get a handle on her out-of-whack hormones. There had to be something wrong. She never had such intense thoughts or feelings before.

Changing the subject would help. What to wear? She went inside and laughed. It wasn't as though she had many choices in the wardrobe department.

Three hours later, they were both ready to go to dinner.

"Are you sure I look okay?" Spring frowned. She hated doubting herself.

"You look fine," Colt replied without looking at her.

"You're a lot of help."

He glanced at her. "Really, you are fine. Let's go." He stepped back gesturing for her to precede him out the door.

Colt opened the truck door for her. He certainly had good manners, and she had to admit she felt exceptional. No one ever opened a car or truck door for her. She needed to stop dissecting every move he made or she'd go crazy. He was a gentleman and that was the extent of it.

There was an easy silence between them as he drove into town. She recognized many of the establishments from applying at most of them. They parked in front of Autumn's Bounty, and as Colt helped her out of the truck, a chill ran through her at his touch. A brief glance at his face confirmed her reasoning was sound; he was only being polite. There was a good crowd in the restaurant. It was beautiful with its gleaming wooden tables and bar. The energy was high, and Spring was instantly glad she came.

A pretty woman jumped up from a table and walked over, smiling at Colt the whole time. Her auburn hair hung loose around her shoulders and her blue eyes sparkled.

Colt pulled her into a big hug. "I've missed you," she whispered as she held onto him.

Spring didn't want to stare but she couldn't glance away either. Maybe they had been more than friends at some point.

Autumn pulled away and took Spring's hand. "I've heard so much about you, and it's a pleasure to finally meet you."

"Thank you it's nice to meet you too." An awkward silence ensued. Damn, she wasn't any good at small talk.

"Well, let me show you to a table." Autumn lead them to a

nice table not too far from the kitchen. "Shall I order up two cactus smoothies?"

Colt laughed. "Darlin', you keep trying but I'm not buying."

Autumn smiled and touched Colt's shoulder. "A girl has to try." She winked at him. "Have a good dinner."

"You two seem close," Spring commented.

"Yes, I suppose we are. I had hoped at one time she'd come to live at the ranch."

"Oh." Spring grabbed the menu, pretending to read it.

"It's not like that. She was pregnant and needed bed rest. I was going to offer, but Jonas beat me to it. They're married now."

"Sorry you lost."

"Spring, look at me." He waited until she lifted her gaze to his. "I never had any permanent intentions toward any woman. If you're afraid I might replace you with someone else, forget it. I won't invite anyone else to come and stay. I'm happy with the work you do."

Grin and bear it, she chanted in her mind. "Of course, that's good to know, and I'm sorry. It's none of my business anyway."

Colt frowned, and she had no idea why. Quickly, she went back to examining the menu. A lump formed in her throat, and she took numerous sips of water to no avail. "It's a great menu; I bet the food is good."

"Oh, I think you'll enjoy it," Autumn said as she approached the table with her arm around an older woman's waist. "This is Peggy Jo your waitress. She's new so give her a break okay?" Autumn smiled and left.

Spring stared at Peggy Jo, it had been a long time since she'd seen her, and she appeared much older than her years. From her grayish complexion to her frizzed, bleached hair, she'd aged considerably since Spring had seen her.

"What are you doing in Carlston? I thought you weren't allowed to leave the state of Texas." Spring arched her brow, waiting for an answer.

"It's so good to see you, honey. It's been far too long, and I've missed you. I found out you moved, so I came here to be near you." The order pad in Peggy Jo's hands shook.

"I didn't think you thought about me at all. How long have you been here?"

"About a week. Everyone here has been so welcoming. You picked a great place to settle down." She smiled but the smile didn't reach her eyes.

"Colt, this is my—um—this is Peggy Jo."

If her emotions hadn't been so high, she would have laughed at the surprise on Colt's face.

He stood and offered his hand. "Ma'am, nice to meet you."

"Likewise. Have you decided what you'd like yet or should I come back?"

Colt sat and gave Spring a questioning glance. "Why don't you come back in a few?"

"Certainly, it really is good to see you, Spring."

The menu suddenly became all-consuming and she stared at it intently. She didn't acknowledge Peggy Jo's comment. When she did glance up, Colt stared at her. "I've only met her a few times. She shoved me into foster care when I was young and every time they tried to terminate her parental rights, she showed up refusing to sign. She made it impossible for me to be adopted. She knew I was being shuffled around from place to place but she didn't care. One time and only one time, I begged her to take me with her. She practically threw me away from her and ran."

Colt reached across the table and took her hand in his, stroking the back of it with his thumb. "I'm sorry, Spring. We can go somewhere else to eat or go home, whatever you want to do."

"I'm not sure I've heard that phrase 'whatever you want to do' said to me before. Thank you for that, and I wouldn't dream of leaving your friend's place. That would be rude."

He squeezed her hand and let go. "She'd understand."

"No, I'm done with that woman, and as far as I'm concerned she just works here."

"Have you had time to decide?" Peggy Jo asked.

"I'll have the pesto linguini with pine nuts and a house salad with blue cheese dressing, oh and coffee." Spring didn't look up the whole time.

"And you, sir?"

"I'll have the same, it sounds good."

Spring waited for Peggy Jo to leave before she gazed at Colt again. The care reflected in his gorgeous brown eyes comforted her, and made her feel less alone. What in the hell was Peggy Jo doing here? She always had an angle, and it was a certainty she had one here.

"You know, I came across the country to start a new life, and the two people I never wanted to see again have found me. It's a bit odd if you ask me."

"Does your mother know Billy?"

She slowly shook her head. "I don't think so. I don't know how they would know each other."

"She's here so you'll have to deal with it the best you can."

"Keeping the least amount of contact possible will be how I will deal with her. I don't want her in my life."

"I don't blame you. Here she comes."

Peggy Jo delivered their salads and gave them both a great big grin. "I'm so happy my girl has found a man like you, Mr. O'Malley. Everyone respects you."

He cleared his throat. "Thank you."

They waited until she left to start eating. Spring nodded as she chewed the first bite. "This is the freshest salad I've ever had."

"Autumn has done wonders with the place. It's busy in here every night, and she has a small baby boy at home."

"Oh wow, a busy woman."

Peggy Jo brought out their pasta and placed the plates in front of them. "Mr. O'Malley, I hear you live on a big ranch. Is your house big?"

Colt shrugged his shoulders. "Big enough I suppose."

"I was so sorry to hear about your loss, Mr. O'Malley. The thing is I've missed my girl, and if you have the room I was wondering—"

They both put down their forks and stared at Peggy Jo. "He's still grieving, and I'm sure Caleb's room is off limits."

"Maybe—"

Colt wiped his mouth with his napkin. "No maybes about it."

Peggy Jo nodded, her disappointment obvious. "Enjoy your meal."

Spring shook her head in disgust. "What did I tell you? She always has some ulterior motive, and she has a lot of nerve asking about your place."

"Let's try to enjoy our food. It's really good."

They finished their pasta in peace until Autumn came over to refill their coffee. "I didn't know Peggy Jo is your mom. Small world. That poor woman has been through a lot in her life. I do have to say I'm surprised, Colt. You refused to put her up at your place? That's not like you at all."

"Spring and her mom don't get along, and right now I need all the peace I can find."

Autumn leaned down and kissed Colt's cheek. "Of course, how insensitive of me. I need to learn to mind my own business."

Colt reached out and held her hand. "You didn't know."

Autumn smiled. "I'll leave you the check and have one of

the other girls take care of it. Spring, it has been a pleasure, and it's nice to know Colt is in good hands."

Spring gave her a graceful nod. "Nice to meet you too."

COLT HAD ORIGINALLY PLANNED to make himself scarce after dinner but now he just couldn't. Wow, Spring's mom was a piece of work. What a pushy woman, and she hadn't even asked her daughter how she was or anything. He saw the hurt, fear and annoyance in Spring's eyes, and it tore at his heart. She was a sweet girl despite having Peggy Jo as a mother.

"You were so quiet on the way home. Are you alright?"

Her shoulders slumped but she nodded. "Just threw me is all. She'll leave sooner than later once she finds that I truly have nothing she wants."

Colt sat on the sofa and stretched out his hand. "Come sit next to me. I want to hear more about this paragon of virtue."

She sat down next to him, as close as she could without touching him. "By the time I was three, I'd been taken away from her three different times. She left me alone all night before I even turned one. That foster family wanted to adopt me immediately, but you know what happened. The second time she regained custody she was driving drunk with me in the car. They took me away for a while and gave me back. The final time she was high, and I wandered into the street. Who knows, they might have given her another chance, but she had moved on to heroin, and she was caught selling. I don't remember much of it. I was around three when she finally went to jail."

She took a deep breath and paused for a moment. "I ended up in the system. I was puny from lack of food so other kids picked on me. I ended up spending a lot of time alone. It seemed as though every time I got comfortable in one home they'd move me to another. Most of the foster parents lost interest when they found out I wasn't adoptable. Then as I grew older, no one wanted to adopt me."

"I remember her visiting me once when she got out of prison. I was about ten or so and she asked me for money. Where would I have gotten any money? I barely had clothes on my back half the time. I had it rough, but I'm stronger for it. I don't expect much and sometimes it's a blessing."

Spring shrugged and gave him a half smile. "I don't trust most people, and I never learned the art of making friends. I was too busy trying to stay under the radar. I tried to be as invisible as possible because I didn't want any trouble. Don't get me wrong, I fought back plenty of times. Didn't win much but I fought back. Then when I was fifteen, Billy came into the picture, and he protected me from the bullies." Chuckling, she shook her head. "I still didn't make any friends, people were too afraid of Billy. I guess my secret wish had always been to have a friend and a little affection. That must be why I never noticed how cruel Billy really was. He asked how my day was and acted interested in what I said. I even shared my hopes and dreams with him."

Colt put his arm around her shoulder and gave it a squeeze. His heart ached for her but he knew better than to show any type of pity.

"The little girl inside me kept waiting for Peggy Jo to get her act together and take me home with her. I kept thinking if I was good enough, she'd come and we'd do all the things real moms and daughters did. We'd go shopping and get ice cream, she'd come to school functions and help me with my homework and she'd hug me."

"Spring—"

"Don't feel sorry for me, Colt. I've had enough of being

that sad little girl. I have my fate in my own hands now, and I'm striving to be happy."

Colt guided her head onto his shoulder. "Honey, I wasn't going to say I feel sorry for you. You are a ray of sunshine around here, and you came just when you were needed most. I'd turned into a shell of myself since Caleb's death. So many people reached out to me but I refused to accept their help. You changed all that, and I'm glad you're here."

The comfort of his warmth soothed her. She snuggled against his shoulder and didn't say anything more. Not long after, her even breathing told him she had fallen asleep.

With great care, he lifted her into his arms and carried her to bed. He finally managed to get her under the covers and was damn surprised she didn't wake. His heart ached for her as he stared at her lovely face. They were just two people trying to find their way, and there was no telling how it would all end up.

MORNING SUNLIGHT POURED into her room as she stretched her arms above her. Her brow wrinkled as she noticed her shoes were still on.

How in the world? She bit back a laugh; Colt must have put her to bed. At least he hadn't taken her clothes off, but shoes? Maybe it was a guy thing, or maybe just a Colt thing.

Talking about her past had been soul-healing. There was a sense of peace around her she'd never experienced before, and it felt great. With Peggy Jo around, it wouldn't last long, so she might as well enjoy it while she could.

While getting ready, she glanced at the mirror. Colt called her lovely. She turned her head to the right then to the left, examining her face. Maybe she wasn't as ugly as Billy told her. Her bright red hair was awful. Autumn's was a nice shade of auburn while hers was too flashy. It had been a curse her whole life. It made her stand out when all she wanted was to go unnoticed. She did have nice skin but she certainly wasn't lovely. Maybe Colt was only trying to make her feel better.

Downstairs Colt already had the coffee on, and he leaned against the counter, mug in hand. She couldn't help but size him up. His hips were slim and his legs well muscled. Her face grew warm as she realized she was staring. When she quickly glanced at Colt's face, he gave her a knowing look. Her face flamed redder.

"Good morning, Spring. Coffee?"

"I'd love some. Funny thing, I woke up with my shoes still on."

Colt poured her coffee and grinned as he handed it to her. Damn, she hated that cocky grin. It was contagious.

"I guess someone found my shoulder a comfy pillow last night. I carried you to bed and tucked you in all without waking you."

"You seem awfully proud of yourself," she teased. "But shoes on in bed?"

"Hell woman, I didn't want to wake you. You looked too damn cute sleeping."

Her smile disappeared. "You don't have to say nice things about how I look."

He cocked his right brow.

"I mean I know I'm plain except for the cursed red hair. I'd rather hear the truth and not some polite compliments."

Colt put his mug down on the counter and stared at her. "I love your red hair, who told you it was a curse?"

She sat at the kitchen table, staring at her coffee cup. "One place I lived they all called me a red headed, freckled faced dog. Billy told me I was nothing to look at. I even remember Peggy Jo bemoaning the fact I had red hair. No one in her family had red hair."

"Do you know who your father is?"

"No, I'm not sure Peggy Jo really knew either."

"It was probably the man with red hair."

She grabbed the towel from table and threw it at him. "Wow, you should have been a detective!"

Colt's deep rumble filled the kitchen as he bent over to retrieve the towel. "Glad to help."

"What's all that?" She nodded toward a disarray of papers, mail and a laptop.

"My bookkeeping. I'll have you know I took a course at the local college."

Her eyes narrowed. "Really? Did they mention organization or are stacks of paper and mail just your style?" She laughed and was heartened at Colt's grin.

"This is my own personal style. I'll have you know it has taken years to perfect it. Now I'll show all you need to know, and you can create your own style. Let's grab our coffee and sit. Do you know what a computer is?"

Shaking her head, she sat at the table next to him. "I'm not sure."

He straightened and turned his computer on. "It takes some getting used to. See all the icons- the pictures- on the left hand side? We will be using these programs to enter the numbers. Now, this little part is the mouse, I know it's a strange name and I still wonder about it. We use the mouse to move the little arrow thing around."

"Oh."

"Exactly, we'll take it slow. Don't get overwhelmed."

It took everything she had not to laugh. Afraid to open her mouth she nodded. It was nice to sit next to Colt. He smelled soap clean with a mix of coffee and leather. She leaned toward him and got as close to him as she could without sitting on his lap.

"Colt, which program are you using for accounting?"

"See this picture? We use that."

"Do you think I could touch your computer?" She smiled and blinked at him.

"Sure." He moved it so it sat in front of her.

She quickly opened his accounting program. "Do you pay your bills online or by check?"

"Online."

"See here? This is an alert of bills outstanding." She clicked the folder. "Dang, Colt, when was the last time you did your bookkeeping?"

His jaw dropped. "You know how to use a computer?"

"Yes, and I took an accounting class in high school. I know the basics." She gave him a wide smile. "You do know it's the twenty-first century don't you?"

He stared at her and shook his head. "This whole time I'm explaining pictures you knew. Why did you let me go on and on?" He huffed in annoyance.

"I like sitting here next to you, and I wanted to prolong it."

"Oh—"

Bibbs walked into the house and smiled. "Hey, I met a woman in town that says she's your mother. A real nice lady. She asked for directions to the ranch."

All laughter and smiles disappeared. "You didn't give them to her, did you?" Spring asked.

Bibbs shook his head. "I did one better, I brought her here. I'll get her."

The door opened, and there stood Peggy Jo, all smiles. Her frizzy bleached hair hung to her shoulders, and she wore skintight jeans with a very low cut top.

Spring cringed. No wonder Bibbs was so willing to give her a ride.

"Colt, dear, your ranch is enchanting." She sauntered toward them. "Spring, honey you must love it here. Reminds me of the place we used to live in. Remember baby?"

Her eyes widened. "No, I don't remember. I do remember rat infested apartments."

"Spring! How could you say that? I always did my best by you. You've landed on your own two feet with a rugged, handsome man, what more do you want?"

Colt cleared his throat. "Spring works for me. Right now, she works for her room and board. Times are tough, and I don't have much, but in a few months, I should be able to pay her a good, living wage. She won't have to rely on me to give her a roof over her head."

"I hope that includes back pay. My baby doesn't work for free." She flipped her hair behind her shoulder.

Spring closed her eyes and bowed her head hoping when she reopened them, Peggy Jo would be gone. "Peggy Jo, this is between Colt and me. I knew what the terms of employment were before I left Texas. It's none of your business."

Peggy Jo blinked a few times and stared at Spring in astonishment. "You knew? Hey, I didn't raise you to be stupid."

Colt stepped forward. "It's time for you to leave. Bibbs take her back to town."

Peggy Jo put her hands on her hips, her eyes flaring. "Oh no, I'm not going anywhere. I came to Montana to live with my daughter and that is what I intend to do. I've been a bit down on my luck lately, and I was hoping for a helping hand."

"No way in hell are you getting one cent from Colt. Just leave." Spring jumped up and began ushering Peggy Jo to the door.

"Let go of me, you have no right. I am your mother!" Peggy Jo screeched.

"Come on, ma'am, it's best I take you home. Emotions are running too high, and the boss wants you gone." Bibbs opened the door and waited for Peggy Jo to precede him outside. He shot an apologetic expression at Spring, and then closed the door.

The moment that woman was out of sight, Spring slumped into her chair, all of her energy drained. What was Peggy Jo thinking coming here? Didn't they make it clear to her she wasn't welcome?

Colt sat down next to her. "I'm sorry, Bibbs didn't know."

"Of course he didn't. Peggy Jo can talk people into anything. She has a knack for manipulation. I just hope she never comes back, but the truth of the matter is she never learns. I have a bad feeling she will be back again since it's obvious she thinks you have money. I'm so sorry, Colt, I just bring bad things to your doorstep."

He reached out, took her small hand in his large work worn one and gave it a quick squeeze. "Don't you worry. I'm pretty sure she got the message this time. I have to admit she has balls coming out here."

"She audaciously pushes through life and surprisingly she gets her way a lot. Well, she won't be back today at least. I just hope she isn't chewing Bibbs' ears off."

"How about we get your mind off her? The paperwork can wait. It's a beautiful day out, and I was thinking that it's time that you learned to ride a horse."

"Ride one? They're actually very tall. Have you ever fallen off?"

Colt chuckled. "Of course I have. It's a part of riding. It depends on the horse's temperament. Some are as gentle as a lamb; others are feisty as all get out. Heidi will be your mount."

"How do you know she's a good horse to ride? I know she's a good mother but…"

"Don't worry, I've been working with her, just for you."

Her face heated. "Really? For me? That's the sweetest thing I've ever heard. She's so tall! I'll never be able to get up on her."

"That's where the handy step-stool comes in."

"Sounds easy enough."

"It'll be fine, and I really think you'll enjoy it."

"Okay, I'm game. Let's go now before I chicken out."

Colt laughed and stood up pulling her up with him. "After you."

She walked straight to the barn, not allowing herself to change her mind. Colt would keep her safe, so what could happen? She could fall off, but she was tough enough to take it. It probably would be fun. "How long will we be gone?"

"Maybe an hour. I'm going to keep us pretty close to the house for your first ride."

She nodded. She could do an hour. She watched as Colt saddled Heavy Duty and Heidi. There was a lot of work involved just getting the horses ready. Colt led them both outside and she followed.

She stood close to Heidi noticing just how much higher Heidi's back was than she'd thought. "Hello, Heidi, we're going for a ride. Be gentle, I'm new."

"Ready?" Colt put the step stool in position and steadied Heidi.

Spring nodded, gritted her teeth and stood on the stool. Now if only Heidi would stop shuffling. She exclaimed in surprise when Colt grabbed her around the waist and lifted her in the saddle. She grabbed the saddle horn so tight her knuckles turned white.

"Here are the reins." Colt tried to hand them to her.

"How can I hold this thing and the reins at the same time?"

"Usually you only hold the reins. Here take them. I'll hold Heidi still."

She took the reins and immediately returned one hand to the saddle horn. "See? I can do both."

Colt grinned. "You'll get the hang of it."

He mounted Heavy Duty and off they went at a very slow walk. Heidi decided to circle one way then the other before she followed the other horse.

They started on a trail, and it wasn't long before Heidi stopped and pulled her head to reach the grass below. Spring pulled the reins, trying to get her to lift her head but to no avail. "Listen Heidi, I can understand the appeal of green grass but we're supposed to be following Colt and you're making me look bad."

Heidi turned her head a bit and then went back to munching.

Finally, Colt turned to see where she was. "Pull the reins up!"

"That's what I've been doing."

Colt rode back to her. "Pull harder, she needs to know you're in control."

"And hurt her poor mouth? I don't think so. She's hungry."

He guided his horse next to Heidi, reached for the reins and pulled. Heidi's head came straight up, and she looked ready to go. "See, it didn't hurt her. It's true you never want to pull too hard. Horses do get hurt that way, but I don't think you're strong enough to hurt a horse. Plus the horse will let you know if it's in pain."

Relieved, she nodded and off they went again. This time she tried to ride holding just the reins until they started up a hill, and she almost went toppling backwards.

"Lean forward!"

"Now you tell me," she grumbled.

"What?"

"Nothing. Just having fun." Surprisingly enough, she was having fun and when the barn came back into view, she wasn't ready for the ride to end.

They rode to the barn, and Colt eased himself out of the saddle. She looked down at the ground wondering how the heck she was supposed to get down. She took her right foot out of the stirrup and tried to slide off only to end up stuck.

"Don't move, Spring." Colt reached up, lifted her out of the saddle and set her down. She was so close to him she could smell him, a scent like leather and earth. Feeling a spark in her stomach, she quickly stepped back. Rejection she couldn't handle today.

"Thank you for taking me. I really enjoyed myself."

Colt stared at her. "You really are lovely. I enjoyed myself too."

There was no way she could hide the smile that spread across her face. "I have things to do inside."

"See you later."

Spring nodded and began to walk away. Her legs were sore and her walk slow.

"Want to go riding again tomorrow?" She knew from the laughter in his voice that he knew she was sore.

"We'll see."

CHAPTER TEN

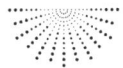

The next day, Colt asked Bibbs about Peggy Jo and was amazed to learn she was now living with Bibbs and Shady.

"Tell me how that happened? What did Shady say?" Colt was wrapping one of the horse's legs.

"I'm not exactly sure. She's really nice and down on her luck. I gave her my room, and I'm on the couch now. Shady likes her too. His girl isn't too happy about the arrangement."

"You gave her your room? Is she paying rent at least?"

"In a couple weeks, she'll start kicking in. The tips at Autumn's Bounty haven't been great."

There was something about the look in Bibbs eyes leading Colt to believe Bibbs had fallen for Peggy Jo. He never imagined that one complication. "Shayla works at Autumn's place, and is raking in the money, at least that's what she told me."

"Well, Shady and I will give it a few weeks and see how it goes." Bibbs did not look like he wanted to hear anything negative about Peggy Jo.

"Hope it all works out for you then. We need to move

some of the cattle down to the pasture past the pond. Here comes Shady. I can't figure why you two don't carpool."

"I refuse to have him drive me anywhere. He's a lead foot, and he thinks I drive like an old biddy. It makes for a better friendship."

"Makes sense to me."

THE WEATHER HAD GOTTEN WARMER, and the sun beat down on the three men. By the end of the day, they were all sweaty and covered in dirt. Shady and Bibbs elected to go home rather than track dirt into the house. Colt waved them off and headed for the house.

He sat on the front porch and pulled off his boots. His jeans were just as bad, and he hesitated before taking them off as well.

Dirt verses embarrassment, what to do? To hell with it. He shucked his jeans and walked into the house.

By the shock on Spring's face, he decided he made the wrong call. Her mouth dropped open, and her face turned bright pink. She stared at his underwear, her eyes widened, and she quickly turned around.

"Sorry, honey, my jeans and boots are covered with mud among other things. It's best to let them dry outside so we can shake most of the dirt off before washing them." Getting no response, he quickened his pace to his bedroom. His body had reacted to her scrutiny, and there was no mistaking what she saw. He was hard as a rock, certainly not a reaction he'd anticipated.

He undressed and stepped into a cold shower, trying to alleviate his problem. It took a while but things went back to normal. It was too hard to deny his attraction and damn near impossible to stay away from her. She drew him to her without even knowing it.

She'd had some bad breaks but she was a survivor, with a heart as big as the Montana sky. He dried himself off and dressed, shaking his head. She didn't want or need a man in her life, and he'd best remember it.

He wandering into the kitchen and had to bite the inside of his cheek to keep from laughing. Spring gave him an assessing look, assessing all of him. Her face turned red, and she twisted her hands.

"I didn't see anything, really. There was nothing to see, I mean..."

He couldn't hold his laughter back any longer. "There was plenty to see, and I hope you're not insulting me by saying it was nothing."

She looked everywhere except at him. "I wasn't looking there."

"Looking where?"

Putting her hands on her hips, she gave him a long glare. "I did not see your great big erection. Is that what you wanted me to say?"

He stopped laughing. "Actually, yes. I was teasing you, and I didn't mean to make you mad. Great big huh?"

"If the sound of your laughter didn't sound so good I'd—well I'd... Heck, I'm going to have to ask Bibbs to give me a list of good threats against you. I never have good come-backs. I think of them later but never when I need them."

"Yep, mean old Bibbs could probably give you quite the list."

She glared at him again.

"Spring, you have no mean factor, even your glare is cute."

She sighed and sat down at the table. "That's me. Too nice for my own good and I still jump at shadows a time or two."

He walked behind her and put his hands on her small shoulders. "I like your niceness, and I happen to think you are one brave woman. You've been through a lot but you aren't cynical or jaded. I'll give you the same advice you gave me: you just be you."

As she turned her head to look at him, he leaned down and kissed her soft cheek. Kissing her lips would have been much nicer but he didn't want her to shy away. Good friends would have to be enough, to bad his libido didn't agree.

———

BEHIND HER CLOSED BEDROOM DOOR, Spring finally relaxed. Yes, she had seen it, yes, she had stared at his erection, and God help her she wanted him. His sly smile all through dinner didn't help her nerves any. You'd think she'd never seen one before! She smiled to herself. It was true she hadn't seen one that looked to be as big as his was. Billy's—she didn't want to waste her time thinking about that creep. A shudder went through her. Hopefully, he was out of her life for good.

Why wouldn't the past just let her go? Enough was enough, especially now with Peggy Jo in town. She never referred to her as mom or mother, because she wasn't. She was simply a thorn in her side who gave birth to her and filled her head with dreams and lies. No matter how Peggy Jo treated her as a child, she waited for Peggy Jo to come back and take her away. A Cinderella story except her prince coming to take her away was Peggy Jo. She'd held tight to her fairytale until right after her eighteenth birthday. She aged out of the system, and for some foolish reason, she expected Peggy Jo to be there waiting to take her home.

Until the ranch, she never felt part of any home. All she knew was distrust and anger. She wasn't a person, just a number. Even in the tiny place where she and Billy lived was never hers. Billy's apartment, Billy's rules.

Here in Carlston with Colt it was different. Here she felt

welcome, and Colt, Bibbs and Shady had become part of her family. They valued her contribution in running the ranch, and they actually seemed to like her. Things would change with Peggy Jo so close; she felt it deep in her heart. That woman was in Carlston to make trouble.

Spring crawled into bed and tried to sleep but it eluded her. The picture of Colt in his underwear would not leave her brain. He did look damn good.

THE NEXT MORNING, Bibbs and Shady arrived by the time Spring had the coffee all ready and was working on bacon. They both smiled and nodded.

"You know where the mugs are help yourself. How are you two this morning?"

Bibbs and Shady exchanged glances and smiled. "We had a home cooked breakfast this morning," Bibbs said.

"Was it good? Which one of you cooked or was it your girlfriend, Shady?"

Both Bibbs and Shady found the floor very interesting all of a sudden. They kept staring at it, shuffling their feet. Finally, Bibbs looked up. "Well you see it was Peggy Jo. She's a mighty fine cook."

She had to have heard wrong. "Did you say Peggy Jo made you breakfast? Is she working at a diner now?"

They filled their mugs with coffee, but they didn't fool her with their little stalling tactic. "Well?"

"Is it true she's your ma?" Shady asked.

Her eyes widened. "Bibbs, do you have something you'd like to tell me? And no, she is not my ma, she might have given birth to me, but she does not have the right to the word ma, mom or mother."

Bibbs grimaced. "Oh hell, I knew it would be this way but Peggy Jo insisted you'd come around. She's staying with

Shady and me. She's had a hard time of it lately and I—we lent a helping hand."

"She's living with you? How big is your bachelor cave?"

Shady turned a bright shade of red. "Two bedroom apartment."

"Which one of you gave Peggy Jo your room?"

Bibbs gasped. "How'd you know? It was me." He hung his head. "She seems like a real nice lady."

"Listen, you can do what you want but I don't want to hear her name ever again."

Shady sipped his coffee, staring at her over the cup rim. "You're not mad at us, are you, Spring? I had no idea."

"No, she has a knack for getting people to do things for her. You are just kind-hearted." She smiled at the relief on both men's faces.

"Come on, Shady. We better go and catch up with the boss."

Shady put down his mug and followed Bibbs. Before they got outside, she heard him ask, "How'd she know about the bedroom?"

"She's smart, that's why."

Chuckling, she shook her head, but her laughter faded beneath a frown before long. Peggy Jo got Bibbs and Shady to take her in? How did that happen?

The front door opened and Colt walked in. "I just heard. Are you okay? Peggy Jo must be some sweet talker to get Bibbs to give up his room."

The concern on his face melted her heart. "She supposedly cooked them breakfast. I don't ever remember her cooking. I just hope she doesn't do too much damage before they end up kicking her out."

"Say the word, and I'll get them to put her out."

She took a deep cleansing breath. This man cared about

her. "No, I don't want any hard feelings. She won't stay long, she never does."

"You didn't answer my initial question." He took a step forward and cupped her face in his hands. "Are you okay?"

"Yes, thanks for asking." She smiled into his eyes.

Colt leaned down and kissed her nose. "Good." He gave her an intense look, then let go.

She watched him walk out the door feeling warm all over. Her lips had begun to tingle in anticipation when he leaned down. A kiss on the nose, what did that mean? She'd never been kissed on the nose before. For the first time, she wished she had a girlfriend she could ask. In fact, her only friends were Colt, Shady and Bibbs. Her entire life had been a lesson in the avoidance of getting close to people.

A couple hours later, Spring heard a knock on the door, and dread filled her. When she opened it, she was immediately assaulted by the woman's powerful perfume. The stranger had magenta hair, and the grim look she sported didn't bode well.

"Good morning. I'm Beverly Rain. I have been remiss not introducing myself to you sooner. I like to get to know all the people in my community."

Spring opened the door wider. "Glad to meet you. I'm Spring, come on in." Spring smiled, wondering what exactly she meant by 'my community' "Can I get you some coffee?"

"Of course, dear." Beverly took off her sweater and scrutinized the house. "Looks nice and clean in here. I'm glad Colt got a maid."

Spring planted a big old fake smile on her face. This wasn't her first go round with this type of woman. There was no way she was going to be baited by this biddy. "Takes a lot of work but it's worth it."

Beverly made herself comfortable on the couch and waited for Spring to bring her coffee.

"Cream or sugar?"

"Black is fine." She took the offered cup. "Thank you."

Spring sat on the plush chair opposite the couch. "What can I do for you?"

Beverly sipped her coffee, stared at Spring and blinked. "Like I said I'm just here to get to know you. I'm considered the matriarch of society in Carlston, and it's my duty to greet all newcomers. Where are you from?"

Greet? It seemed more like an interview. "I'm from Texas."

"Oh? How'd you end up here on the O'Malley ranch?"

"Caleb invited me to come work here. Unfortunately I wasn't aware of his passing before I arrived."

"What an awful reminder of Caleb it must be to Colt, having you underfoot." There was a squint to Beverly's eyes as she smirked.

"I'm not sure about that. You'd have to discuss that with Colt. I don't talk about my employer's." Spring smirked back.

"I see, well maybe you can tell me why you kicked your sweet mother out into the street? Poor Bibbs and Shady had to take her in. It's a disgrace if you ask me. Here in Carlston we believe family takes care of family." She raised her misshapen eyebrows and tilted her head.

Spring put on her blank, emotionless mask. She tightened her lips to keep from screaming at the nosey old bat. Standing, she whisked Beverly's coffee cup away and headed into the kitchen. She put the cup in the sink and slowly turned around. "It was so nice to meet you, Mrs. Rain." She went to the door and held it open.

"It's Miss not Mrs.," Beverly replied in a huff as she walked toward the door.

"What a surprise. You have yourself a great day, and bless your heart."

Beverly walked out the door and hesitated on the

doorstep. She appeared a bit perplexed, and Spring wanted to laugh, but she shut the door instead.

Now if Beverly had been from Texas, she'd know what 'bless your heart' really meant, and she'd know what Spring really wanted to tell her.

Colt barged into the house his face full of worry that quickly changed into relief. "You're laughing? Beverly has been known to make people cry."

"Believe me she tried. That queen of society won't be inviting me to any socials."

Colt groaned. "What did you do?"

"I told her I don't discuss my employers and when she gave me a lecture about being nice to Peggy Jo and family being important I took her coffee away and held the door open. I even said bless your heart. See, I was nice."

A deep laugh echoed throughout the house. "Caleb had told me about you sassy Texans and your heart blessing. Now I know why you're laughing. It's nice to hear you laugh, you don't do it often enough."

"Neither do you." They stared into each other's eyes and fell quiet for a time.

"I want to kiss you, Spring." His voice had turned husky.

"Will it mean something this time?"

"This time? Oh, the kiss in the barn. That was a mere peck. I'm talking about a real kiss."

"I thought—"

"Don't think. It gets us in trouble when we think. I just end up putting my foot in my mouth and making you mad."

"Who said I was mad?"

"It's not easy to tell what you feel half the time."

"Well, it was a necessity when I was young. You know how they say in prison, 'you should keep your head down, eyes open and mind you own business'? It's the same principle really."

"I'm sorry."

"Don't be sorry, it's done, and I made it out of there. Most end up on drugs or dead. I do have to thank Billy that I'm still sane. Sometimes I don't know how to feel or act, but I'm learning."

Colt nodded. "You'll be fine. You're a survivor and a fighter." He put his hat back on and walked to the door. He grabbed the knob and turned back giving her one of his killer smiles. "I still want to kiss you."

Before she could answer, he was out the door. She was half-afraid if she wanted him, he'd be taken away, just like a toy. It was best not to hope too much. In the end, it hurt less.

As for that Beverly woman, it stung that she'd prejudged Spring before meeting her. How dare she act so high and mighty, especially where Peggy Jo was concerned? Damn, Peggy Jo must be putting on some act and raising sympathy from the town.

Her thoughts kept whirling, wondering why Peggy Jo had really come to Carlston. Going stir crazy, she walked outside and headed for the barn. She entered the barn, and there was Bibbs sporting a big old smile. "Hi, Bibbs."

"Hey, darlin'. What's up?"

Had he gotten his hair cut and his beard shaped? He didn't seem so Grizzly Adams now. "I thought I'd get to know the horses a bit. I never was around many animals before, and Colt just loves horses." She trailed off not knowing what else to say.

"Let me give you the grand tour," Bibbs offered.

Nodding, she drew closer to him. "Where does the tour start?"

"I'll introduce you to the horses."

"The rescue horses?"

"Aww, some of those poor souls might scare you." Bibbs frowned.

"I'd really like to see the rescue horses and learn what a horse rescue really means."

He studied her for a moment then nodded. "Follow me."

They stopped in front of the closest stall. "Now, most of the time we don't know the horse's name. It depends on how we obtain them. Mostly we do everything we can to get them well and out of abusive situations." He nodded toward the horse in the stall. "This is Railroad, we bought him at auction."

"Oh wow, he's a bag of bones. Auction?"

"Most likely whoever bought him would just sell him over the border for slaughter. We keep our eyes out for these sad beings. There's a list on the internet we check daily for horses being sold for little to no money."

"Why would an owner sell for such low prices?"

"I figure they don't want to pay to feed the animals and don't want to have to dispose of a dead body so they practically give them away to avoid the cost."

She gasped. "It doesn't make sense to me. I don't get it. So Railroad was being starved?"

Bibbs stroked his gray beard. "Looks that way. On the bright side, he's here now and Colt will do his best to get him healthy and into a forever home. Colt and Caleb started this project years ago and boy, they had no idea how many horses needed their help. Jonas Barnes takes in the worst cases, he does what he can but most don't make it. I couldn't do what he does, watch horses die, but he says he wants the horses to know all people aren't cruel before they go. Stone McCoy takes in the overflow, and now we have Holden. He's a vet and donates his time and medicine."

"It must be expensive for everyone involved."

"That's why we run cattle. It pays for the expenses."

"Railroad," she called softly.

The horse looked her straight in the eye then turned away.

"I can see his ribs."

Bibbs nodded. "He's eating though, and that's a good sign."

"What's a 'forever home'?"

"You know how people adopt cats and dogs? It's the same thing. Colt does a background check and goes out to see where the horse will live. He's very particular and does his best by these horses."

"He's a good man."

"That he is, aren't you, Boss?"

Spring spun around, and there was Colt leaning against a stall not far away. "I try." He smiled at her, and her heart flipped in her chest.

"Did you want to go riding again today?" Colt asked with laughter in his voice.

She would have bristled at his poking fun, but her legs and rear end hurt too much to indulge his challenge. "Thanks for asking but there are parts of me that are still sore from our last ride."

Bibbs winked at her and left the barn.

"Oh?" Colt slowly edged toward her. "And what parts might those be?"

It was an electrical charge emanating from him, and if he came any closer, she'd be done for. "Did Bibbs get a haircut? His beard isn't as ragged either."

Colt chuckled. "He thinks he's courting your—I mean Peggy Jo."

The playful atmosphere disappeared. "I was afraid of that. He's going to end up hurt."

"I talked to him, and it's what he wants to do." He shrugged. "He's old enough to know his own mind."

"You really do great work with the horses. I never knew there were so many."

"I just wish there were more owner-surrenders instead of us having to go in and take the abused horse."

"How did you get started?"

He rubbed the back of his neck and stared at Railroad. The silence lengthened between them. "My dad almost beat a horse to death. I went to the police but at the time, it wasn't against the law. The horse was his property. I snuck old Gumbo over to Jonas' place. We were both in high school at the time, and his dad was kind enough to let me keep Gumbo there. I went over every day and made sure Gumbo ate and his wounds were tended. Jonas was a big help too. My dad punched me in the face when he heard about it. It was that moment I decided I was not going to allow horses to be abused." He glanced at her. "I had no idea how much need there was for rescues."

"I admire what you do."

"I have to tell you, I'll never be a rich man. Most of my money goes to the horses."

"You are rich; you have an abundance of caring. You're gentle and honest and the fact you don't expect to be repaid amazes me."

"I do sell the horses to their new owners, but I don't charge much. It doesn't even cover expenses. I just want them to have a good home."

Wistfulness invaded her. "Why don't they have rescues for people? What about the children in the system who never really have a chance?"

"I wish I had an answer for you, Spring."

CHAPTER ELEVEN

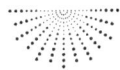

*I*t was going to be an extremely hard day, and Colt hoped he could make it through without breaking down. It was Caleb's birthday, and the pain that never left magnified. A trip to the cemetery was in order, and he dreaded it. There were times he just pretended Caleb was away at college, and he'd still be coming home. Then there were the days he woke up, and the first thought in his head was his brother was dead. It was as though a part of him was missing, and he didn't know how to adjust.

It had been a few months now. He should be over it and moving on. That's how it was portrayed on television. Hell, according to some stuff he'd watched, he should have gone on with his life, feeling happy by now. Everyone goes through it at some point, and they all seemed fine. What was wrong with him?

Feeling weary and old, he got out of bed and dressed. Caleb wouldn't mind if he didn't shave. He almost smiled thinking about it. He taught Caleb to shave. That pain in his chest only grew. He'd taught Caleb just about everything except for knowing when not to be a hero. Maybe Caleb wouldn't have gone searching for Snoopy if he hadn't instilled in him the importance of being kind to animals.

Spring stared at the kitchen table looking fresh and young. He walked closer, wondering if he ever looked as young anymore.

"Good morning." She jumped up and poured his coffee. "I'll have breakfast ready in a snap."

"I'm not hungry this morning, honey. Coffee will do it."

She gave him a long accessing look. "Out with it, what happened? Was it Peggy Jo?"

Colt sat and stared at his cup. Finally, he sighed. "No, it's Caleb's birthday today. He would have been twenty- two and finishing up college this year."

Her hand flew to her mouth then she slowly approached him and dropped her hand on his shoulder. "I'm so sorry, Colt."

He turned his head and gazed at her. "You'll be fine?"

"Will I live? Yes. Will I be fine? No. There is so much of Caleb in everything on this ranch. I think about him every day, and I mourn him. However, I'm so grateful to have known him. If not for him, I'd probably be lying in a hospital by now, if I were still alive. I suppose it was the same caring heart that sent me here and went out into the storm to find a little girl's dog."

"Maybe I shouldn't have allowed him to care so much. There must have been something I could have done." He shrugged her hand off his shoulder and gazed into her blue eyes. The concern he glimpsed in them touched him. For someone who never showed her feelings before, she was transparent now. "I'm going to the cemetery, would you join me?"

"I'd be honored to go with you."

"Good, meet me at the truck in fifteen?"

Spring nodded, and he headed outside to the barn. There

was a horseshoe in the tack room Caleb had hung years ago claiming it would bring them luck. He planned to leave it at Caleb's grave. Maybe it wasn't so lucky after all, but Caleb had proudly nailed it up above the doorframe. It was better than flowers. Caleb was not a flower person. He'd like the horseshoe though.

Spring was leaning against the truck when he left the barn. He liked people who were punctual. Opening the truck door for her, he caught her scent of flower blossoms, nice and sweet like her. He wondered how mad she'd get if he called her sweet, and it was enough to make him smile momentarily.

The drive was quiet, all of his thoughts on missing Caleb. His heart twisted as they got closer, and by the time he parked, he was in agony. If there was a heaven then Caleb was certainly there, hopefully happy. Agony was for the living, the ones left behind.

They got out of the truck, and a gentle wind brushed past. The sun was shining, and the grass at the cemetery was a nice shade of green. He remembered picking out the plot. There had been so many details; he thought he'd lose his mind. Looking at the beautiful view of the mountains, he knew he'd made the right choice. "It's this way."

Spring followed silently, looking lost in thought.

"He's right here." Colt stopped in front of the granite grave marker. "I liked this spot because the statue of Jesus was close by. This is the first time I've been back here."

"It certainly is a beautiful spot. He would have liked it. I'm going to walk around and give you time alone with your brother."

"Thanks." He wasn't sure he wanted to be alone, but before he knew it, she was gone.

Grief he couldn't push back down welled up inside him. "Happy Birthday, Caleb. I miss you, a lot, more than I ever thought possible. It's been hard to go on without you, but thank you for sending Spring to me. Somehow, she makes the days bearable. I'm finally getting back into a routine. There have been many horses that have needed my help lately. I'd give anything to have you back, but life doesn't work that way, and we both know it." He knelt down on one knee, removed his hat and placed the horseshoe on Caleb's grave. "I figured you'd rather have this than some flowers. Happy Birthday, buddy."

He stood back up and watched Spring walk toward him. He really would have lost his sanity if not for her.

"I have something I want to leave for Caleb." She pulled a light green marbled rock out of her pocket. "He gave this to me one day. I kept it in my work locker. I didn't want to take a chance Billy would take it away." She held the rock for him to examine. "It says Joy on it. When he sent me here, he gave me real joy. Your ranch is beautiful, and I love working there."

She knelt in front of Caleb's grave and placed the rock on the grave marker. "Thank you, Caleb and happy birthday my friend."

Colt reached out his hand to help her up, and it felt so right to have her hand in his. Her blue eyes mirrored his sorrow, and it gave him comfort to know he wasn't alone.

THREE DAYS later Spring was on her way out to the barn. She went there every day now to see the horses. A car speed up the driveway, and as it got closer, it surprised her it was a police car. Hopefully, more horses weren't in trouble.

The sheriff jumped out of the car and came barreling toward her. His piercing eyes were frightening. "I'm Sheriff Brown, and I need you to come with me."

Her eyes widened, and her jaw dropped. "What? Why would you need me to go with you?"

"Peggy Jo is pressing assault charges against you. I need to take you to the station, and you can call a lawyer from there."

"I've only seen Peggy Jo twice, when she first came to town and that is all!"

He smirked at her. "See, you didn't deny the assault charges, and if you were innocent you would have done that first. You don't fool me, sweetheart. Colt might be a sucker for a pretty face but I knew you were bad news when Beverly told me about her visit to you."

He grabbed her shoulder, and she jerked away, ready to run. Unfortunately, she hesitated and before she knew it, he'd slapped handcuffs on her. "Colt!"

Before she could call out again, Sheriff Brown pushed her into the back seat and slammed the door shut. The pounding of her heart was her only tell, otherwise her façade was blank. The only way to get through this was to remain calm.

Damn Peggy Jo! What was she after and who beat her up? It wasn't the first time Peggy Jo's face was black and blue. Her mouth never stopped, and she'd made more than one crazy man furious enough to hit her.

"You seem awfully calm back there, missy. Jail is not a fun place you know."

Spring could see his taunting eyes in the rear view mirror. What was this guy's game? Assault charges were no big deal, comparatively. What was Beverly's take in all this? Nosy old bat.

Her heart began to slow to a normal rate. She knew they had nothing on her; hopefully, she'd be home by dinner.

He pulled into a small parking lot. She didn't remember seeing a jail when she was in town looking for a job. She recognized the animal clinic nearby and wondered if Mindy Sue might look outside to see her. The back door jerked open, and the sheriff pulled her, none too gently, out of the car.

He grabbed her arm and led her into the back of the community center, an interesting combo. She peacefully walked where he wanted. The first thing she saw in the small police station was Peggy Jo crying into a tissue with Beverly Rain comforting her. The urge to roll her eyes was overwhelming but she put on an expression of concern.

"Peggy Jo, that looks awful. Have you gone to the doctor or the hospital?"

Both Peggy Jo and Beverly glared at her. Peggy Jo sniffed. "Like you care, you horrible child."

Both the sheriff and Beverly nodded in agreement, and Spring felt her first glimmer of fear. She was pushed into an interrogation room and told to sit down.

"Could you take the handcuffs off? They hurt."

He took a key out of his pants pocket and unlocked one hand, then the other.

"I'd like to make a phone call." She stared him down.

"I haven't arrested you, so no phone call. You're here to be interrogated."

"About?"

"You are a cold one, Spring Reed. Smacking someone around like that, even your mother, is a crime." His voice became louder with each word.

"In that case, I'd like a lawyer please." She took a deep breath and tried to keep the calm serene expression on her face.

"A lawyer? You've been in trouble with the law before haven't you? You think you know the ins and outs? You have no idea of my reach in the law enforcement community. I'm well known. If I want to throw you in jail and throw away the key I can."

"Well, can I talk to a lawyer first? I'd hate for you to break the law."

His face grew red. "I'll have to see if there is one available, might take some time." He opened the metal door and slammed it behind him.

Jackass. He was full of himself, and his reach in the law enforcement community. Feeling a smile coming on, she pressed her lips together and stared right into the two-way mirror. How many people were watching her? Peggy Jo, Beverly perhaps?

It didn't matter, it was a waiting game now, and if they thought they scared her, they were mistaken. She'd grown up in hell and sitting here was nothing compared to that.

No LUNCH? Colt's eyebrows furrowed as he wondered where Spring was. He'd already looked around the house, and he'd just come from the barn. She probably went on one of her walks or something. He pulled all the fixings for sandwiches out of the refrigerator. They'd just make their own sandwiches, no big deal.

The door opened and Shady and Bibbs walked in. "Is Spring sick?" Shady asked, eyeing the old sandwich fixin's.

Colt shrugged his shoulders. "No, she was fine this morning. I don't know where she is now though."

"It is a nice day out," Shady commented with a shrug.

Bibbs turned white. "I had to throw Peggy Jo out of our place yesterday after work. She was always drunk, but yesterday she had drugs on her so I kicked her out. Do you think something happened to her and Spring had to go?"

"I doubt it Bibbs. Spring has no way to get anywhere and plus she would have asked one of us to drive her. Make a sandwich, she'll be back soon."

Colt was not concerned about Spring until he came home for dinner, and she still was gone. He flagged Shady and Bibbs down before they left.

"What's up, Boss?" Shady asked.

"Spring is still missing. Do you think you can take the ATV and look around the property? Bibbs, where was Peggy Jo hanging out?"

"The bar at Frank's Place mostly. Want me to check it out?"

"I'd appreciate it, thanks guys. I'm going to drive to town and glance around. Keep in touch and Shady, be careful."

Shady gave him a lopsided grin. "Of course."

So sure of himself, just like Caleb. Colt sighed and headed toward his truck. Where could she have gone? Maybe Peggy Jo overdosed or something. He quickly dismissed that idea, someone would have called him. At least she hadn't packed her things. What if he was wrong to look in town? Maybe she took a walk and was lost or hurt. If so, Shady would find her, he told himself. It was his job to check town. He gunned the engine and drove faster.

Hell, he didn't even have a game plan, but driving around town seemed as good a plan as any.

He made one pass through town and decided to park and walk. The town wasn't very big; it only had one traffic light. He tried Lucy's Deli, the Food Mart, Carlton Diner, and no one had seen her. Finally, he stopped at Autumn's Bounty. Autumn wasn't there, but Shayna Lowerly, the new manager, was.

Colt frowned as Shayna explained how she had to fire Peggy Jo the other day, and how there was a rumor Spring beat Peggy Jo to a pulp. As soon as he heard, he hightailed it out of there and headed for the town jail. Damn that useless sheriff, if he laid one hand on Spring… He just needed to see she was fine.

He walked into the police station, and Sheriff Brown was sitting at his desk eating fried chicken.

He smiled at Colt and licked his fingers clean. "Something I can help you with? Another horse need saving? I already told you animal control is who you contact."

"Have you seen Spring?"

"Spring Reed?"

"Yes, Spring Reed." Colt gritted his teeth. He wasn't in the mood for games.

"She's in the interrogation room, has been for about six plus hours now."

Colt clenched and unclenched his hands. "Why?"

"She wants a lawyer, so she'll have to wait until I locate one."

"How many have you called?" Colt growled.

"I haven't had a chance yet. It's been a busy day and all." The sheriff smirked.

"I would like to see her."

The sheriff tipped his chair back. "No can do. No one can talk to her until she gets a lawyer."

Colt glared at him. "Well, it just so happens I have a cousin in the next town over who is a lawyer."

"I don't know any lawyer named O'Malley."

Colt grabbed his phone out of his pocket and quickly called his cousin then he turned toward the sheriff. "She'll be right here. For some reason she really doesn't like you." Colt grinned.

"What's her name?"

"Diane, Diane Byrne."

Sheriff Brown stopped smiling. "I don't want that bitch anywhere near this office."

"Not your choice. I have a few calls to make. I'll sit outside until she gets here.

SPRING WONDERED how long she'd been sitting in the interrogation room. There were no clocks, and she didn't have a watch. The damn sheriff was being an ass. He must think her stupid with his little ploys to get her to talk to him. First, he turned the heat up until she sweated, and now it was so cold she was shivering. He asked her if she wanted something to drink but she refused because he probably wouldn't allow her to use the restroom. She'd known plenty of people who had been arrested and she'd heard all the stories. One boy came back from the police with bruises on him when she was a kid. She was better off waiting him out. She even tried to take a short nap, but Brown banged on the metal door asking her if she was okay. If he'd yelled any louder, the whole town would have heard him.

There had been no mention of a lawyer, and she was beginning to doubt he even called one. Did Colt know? Would he believe the allegations?

She crossed her arms in front of her. At least the handcuffs were off so she could try to warm herself. Pacing helped with her growing frustration. When was she supposed to have hit Peggy Jo? She'd been on the ranch the whole time. Though sorely tempted to talk to the sheriff and get it all over with, she knew better. No phone call? That probably was the law but it still didn't seem right.

Now she wished she'd paid more attention to the delinquents she'd lived with. Could he keep her here overnight? There was a time limit but she wasn't sure what that limit was. It could be a certain number of hours or a day. Billy would know. She chuckled bitterly for a moment. Billy was the one she pictured being in trouble with the law but never her.

Really, what did Peggy Jo have to gain by accusing her?

She never could understand that woman.

The door finally swung open, and in walked a well-dressed woman with long white hair and brown eyes. "Are you okay?" She put out her hand. "I'm Diane Byrne, your lawyer."

Spring shook her hand. "I don't have money for a fancy lawyer."

Diane smiled. "I'm Colt's cousin, and cousins do for each other."

"Thanks for coming." Spring smiled back. She had no idea what the whole "cousins do for each other" was about, but it warmed her that Colt sent Diane.

They both sat down at the table, and Diane pulled out a notebook and pen from her leather briefcase.

"Now how do you know Peggy Jo Hobbs?"

"Hobbs? Is that the name she goes by now? It doesn't matter. She gave birth to me."

"And? I need as much info as possible to get you out of here. I don't know what you did to old Brownie out there, but he's gunning for you."

Another smile graced Spring's face at the insult to the sheriff. "She—well I was taken from her when I was a toddler, and she's been briefly in and out of my life since. She's an addict. I believe heroin is her drug of choice. I've been in the foster care system most of my life. She's always lived in Texas until she showed up a few weeks ago at a restaurant here and then at Colt's place. She expected to live there, which makes no sense to me. I didn't tell her or anyone else where I was living. Bibbs, one of the men who works for Colt—"

"I know Bibbs. Nice guy."

"He is. Anyway, he offered to put her up at his place. That was the last I heard until I was picked up this morning."

Diane shook her head. "You've been here all day?"

Spring nodded her head and shrugged her shoulders. "I refused to talk to the sheriff without a lawyer. He said he'd call one."

"Yeah right, he probably left a message on a lawyer's machine who he knew was out of town. Never liked Brownie and never will. I've tried over the years to get him run out of office but so far no luck. What did he say to you?"

"That Peggy Jo accused me of assault, and when we got here, she and the Beverly woman were here waiting. Someone beat her but it wasn't me."

"Beverly is mixed up in this?"

"She took it upon herself to inform me I'm supposed to take care of my mother by allowing her to live at the ranch. She's not a big fan of mine."

"Do you have an alibi?"

"I was at the ranch all week. The bruises do look fresh but I was home. And I don't have a way to get into town."

Diane nodded, stood up and opened the door. "Come on in, Brownie."

He barged into the room, his face red. "I told you not to call me that," he hissed.

"Let's get to the business at hand." Diane stared the sheriff down. "My client has been left in here all day on the word of a junkie? Maybe her drug dealer beat her up. From what I've heard, she was fired from her job and kicked out of the apartment due to her drug use. Makes more sense to me she couldn't pay her supplier."

"She claims her daughter did it. How many moms do you know who turn their kids in unjustly?" The glimmer of triumph on his face had Spring's hand itching to slap it.

Diane took a deep breath and let it out slowly as though she was trying to maintain her cool. "First of all Peggy Jo may have given birth to Spring, but she has never been her mother. Spring has grown up in the foster system because

Peggy Jo is a junkie. Why she moved to Carlston I have no idea, but I bet if you run their names through the system you'll find Spring has a clean record while Peggy Jo has a colorful one. And one more thing, you might want to be sure Hobbs is her real last name."

"But Beverly—"

"Did you lose your balls again, Brownie? That woman's gossip is not to be trusted. When will you ever learn?"

He glared at them both. "I'm not convinced, and I can keep her for forty-eight hours, which in this case is appropriate."

"Playing hard ball? Judge Andrews is waiting for my return call on how this little matter turns out."

"Don't you threaten me you old—"

"Tsk, tsk, Brown. Did I mention she has an alibi? Yeah, she was on the O'Malley ranch with Colt. I happen to know you already heard this information."

"Hell, get out of here, both of you." He pointed his finger at Spring. "You'd better not leave the county."

Diane smiled. "She'll be at Colt's. Nice to see you again, Sheriff Brown." She opened the door and gestured to Spring to go out first.

The air outside the room was much warmer, and it felt good as Spring walked toward the front door. Colt stood near the door, and as soon as he spotted her, his frown turned into a bright smile.

"Diane got you sprung?" His voice was husky and full of concern.

She nodded and walked into his embrace. She never had anyone go to such lengths to help before. Her emotions finally got to her, and she hugged Colt tight for a few long minutes. Reluctantly, she let go but she kept her gaze averted. Letting her guard down still scared her.

Colt hugged Diane next. "Thanks for coming to the

155

rescue, Cuz. I can give you a horse as repayment." He laughed and his eyes sparkled.

Diane stepped out of his embrace and punched his shoulder. "I've taken all the horses off your hands I can handle, and you know it. Let's get out of here before Brownie makes more trouble."

They hustled out the door into the cool night air. Colt immediately took his jacket off and put it over Spring's shoulders. She smiled briefly, trying her damnedest to get on an even keel after the mess that was her day.

"Thank you Diane, I'm so grateful you came to help me. I wasn't sure anyone knew where I was."

"My pleasure, and you call if that jerk gives you any more trouble." She kissed Colt's cheek and hurried to her car.

Colt took her hand and entwined his fingers with hers. "I would have been here sooner, but to tell you the truth I didn't even know you were gone until dinner time. You were missing before lunch, but I figured you were around somewhere."

She followed his lead to his truck. "Not your fault. No one could have guessed I'd been brought in for questioning. Did you know if you're not arrested you don't get a phone call?"

They got into the truck, and Colt started to drive toward the ranch. "I'm not up on the ins and out of being arrested. I'm just glad we found you."

"We?"

"Bibbs went looking for Peggy Jo, never did find her. Shady went out on the ATV to check the property. I originally thought you went looking for flowers again."

A pleasant warmness sprung up inside her. No one had bothered to look for her before. At least not out of concern. It was nice they truly cared about her. "I appreciate that y'all took the time to look for me."

Colt glanced at her. "Was there any doubt we'd eventually find you?"

She wasn't sure how to answer. It wasn't doubt so much as it was the norm for her. Of course, she'd hoped he would come, but she hadn't expected it. "I'm just glad you found me."

He reached over and gave her hand a quick squeeze. "I'm just glad you're alright. Though I would like to know why Peggy Jo accused you."

"Maybe she thinks you have money after all."

Later that night as she lie awake in bed, her conflicting emotions made it hard to sleep. If she was going to be honest, it was damn near impossible to sleep. Peggy Jo made her sick and wary, Billy scared her, Bibb's and Shady's friendship filled her with warmth and her heart melted with need for Colt. The need wasn't totally sexual, the need encompassed their whole relationship and her desire for closeness. Some of the emotions were so familiar and some perplexed her. Lately he seemed to draw her to him, and she didn't want to fight it anymore. There was everyday proof he was a good, honest, gentle man whom she could count on, and she finally believed in him.

A relationship with Colt? Why not? It scared her to death, but she could be fearless when necessary, couldn't she? If things didn't work out, she'd be out of a job and a place to live, but by then, she could be self-sufficient. She'd allowed her head to make all decisions in her life so far. She wasn't sure how to lead with her heart.

Sighing, she turned over. Peggy Jo was crazy, but she usually had a reason for doing things. Accusing her of assault had to be the worst thing she'd ever done. Okay, maybe not the worst, but it was right up there, and she needed to find out what that woman was planning.

Her mind whirled until she finally fell into a fitful sleep.

CHAPTER TWELVE

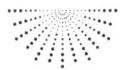

The next day Colt spent a good amount of time with Railroad. He was a well-mannered gelding and had a great appetite. He would be an asset to any horse lover. Sometimes it was hard to turn a horse around after they'd been abused, but he rarely gave up. Placing the horses with loving owners was important.

Keeping the ranch in good shape for Caleb had been his goal, and it was time to set a new one. Honestly, he'd been thinking about a family. Kids might be a good thing, and he was hoping Spring might fit into his new goal. She'd been more affectionate and less bristly lately, and he enjoyed it. He liked her company; she was smart and a hard worker. What more could he ask for? Well, of course, he found her sexy as hell too, and his plan was to lull her into wanting to touch him and be with him. Just like gentling a horse.

He chuckled, and Railroad turned his head to stare at him. "What? Can't a guy have a happy moment?" His smile disappeared with his revelation. Spring made him happy, surprisingly happy, and he never thought to be happy again.

"Hey, Boss, you okay?" Shady asked as he swaggered into

the barn. "You sure look puzzled. The food goes into the horse's mouth, hope it helps."

A deep laugh bubbled up, and Colt couldn't stop laughing. The more Shady stared at him the more he laughed. "It's been so long since I had such a good laugh like that. Thanks kid."

"I don't think you hear half the things I say. I'm funny a good portion of the time."

Colt put Railroad back into his stall, patted his neck and walked out of the barn with a huge grin on his face. Shady must be delusional, he was usually anything but funny.

Walking into the house, he still slightly chuckled. Spring was on a ladder cleaning windows, and she looked delicious. Life wasn't a guarantee. Caleb's death hammered that into him. There wasn't time for regrets and chances didn't always come like this. He knew that now.

Spring glanced over her shoulder and grinned. In her eyes, he spotted happiness and it warmed him. In two long strides, he was beside the ladder. She gingerly turned on the steps as he reached his arms up to her. The way her face lit up gave him the confidence he needed to scoop her up and hold her against him.

"What are you doing?" She laughed as he put her down but he didn't let go.

"I've had something on my mind for a while now." He studied her dusty pink lips.

"What would that be?" Her voice was husky.

Leaning down, he kissed her and as soon as his tongue touched her lips, she opened for him. Groaning, he deepened the kiss and was thrilled when she put her arms around his neck to pull him closer.

Spring squirmed against him while they kissed. Her kisses were feverish as though she couldn't get enough, and her tongue tangoed with his in a sexily charged dance. No one had ever kissed him with such passion.

He lifted her until she wrapped her long legs around his waist. They stared at each other. Was he going too fast? When she started to kiss the side of his neck, his question was answered. He set her down on the kitchen counter and quickly took care of her shirt and bra. Her exposed breasts were sheer perfection topped with pink nipples begging for attention.

Standing between her legs, he leaned down and kissed each nipple then he rolled them between his thumb and finger. Her squeals of delight urged him on. He kissed her neck leaving a trail all the way back to her breasts. How he wanted her with everything he was. Before he knew it, she had his shirt opened, and her dainty hands on his hard chest sent sparks through him.

Just as she started kissing his chest, the door opened, and they both jumped.

"Guess this isn't a good time for coffee," Bibbs said. He turned and walked out the door.

Their laughter filled the house, and at that moment, he knew he had to have her as his wife. No one ever made him feel the way she did. No one. However, the time wasn't right.

Spring began to button his shirt, and she laughed at his frown. "How much do you want to bet Shady isn't far behind?"

Grabbing her bra and shirt, he handed them to her. "You're right. Those two are the nosiest cowboys I know."

She dressed and ran her fingers through her long red hair. "I guess I got carried away."

He placed his finger over her lips. "No, it was amazing, and I guess you can't imagine how you make me feel. No regrets or second thoughts. In fact it was the best kiss I'd ever had."

Her eyes shimmered as she swallowed hard. She nodded and met his gaze. He got a rare glimpse into her heart, and it invigorated him with hope for their future. In that moment, he wanted to grab her up and take her to bed, but he knew he wanted to handle her with care. He now had no doubts they'd get there eventually.

SPRING TOUCHED HER LIPS, smiling. Just as she predicted, Shady came in for coffee. The disappointment on his face had her and Colt laughing. They laughed even harder when Shady left without any coffee.

Everything was different with Colt, and she didn't feel a moment of shame or fear kissing him. Maybe getting involved with the man she worked for wasn't the wisest thing, but her feelings for him were too strong to deny any longer.

The windows wouldn't clean themselves, however, and once again, she climbed the ladder and took up her cloth. Finally, she was cleaning the last window in the back part of the house. The sun was at such an angle it was almost blinding, but she was determined to finish. Looking out, she saw someone standing near a cluster of evergreens. She placed her hand above her eyes to shield her eyes from the sun, but she still couldn't get a good look. Muscles knotting in her stomach told her it had to be Billy, and her gut was usually right.

Quickly, she got off the ladder and ran out the back door. To her dismay, no one was there. She cautiously walked over to the trees and glanced around but there was no sign of anyone. Shaking her head, she let out the breath she hadn't realized she was holding.

As she turned to walk back, she spotted a cigarette butt

saw smoke. I tried to call you, and I called the sheriff's office. Then I thought about you being out here alone and…"

Colt pulled her close. "You're shaking. Let's get you back into the house."

Nodding, she allowed Colt to lead her. Terror filled her; afraid that somehow Billy was there. "What if he's in here?"

Colt locked the door and searched the house quickly and quietly. Then he called Bibbs giving him a heads up. "He's not here, honey. You shouldn't have taken a chance warning me." He grabbed her hand and pulled her into an embrace. "I'm sorry, I shouldn't have let security get so lax."

In the circle of his arms, she felt safe, and her heartbeat slowed to a normal rhythm. "I wasn't thinking either when I went outside to see who was out there."

"Are you sure it was Billy?"

"Who else would it be? Something hit the side of the house; I couldn't see what it was."

Colt stroked her back. "The sheriff is on his way?"

"I doubt it. Are Bibbs and Shady on their way back? You told them to be careful right?" "Take a deep breath. You heard me on the phone with Bibbs. They'll be careful." Colt guided her to the couch and sat next to her. "Why don't you think the sheriff is coming?"

"The woman who answered the phone asked if I was the one who hit Peggy Jo. She did say she'd radio the sheriff, but she hung up on me. Colt, Billy is dangerous, but I won't allow him to hurt the people I love. If I go, he goes."

"Love?" His chocolate eyes widened as he stared at her.

"Well, yeah, I think of you, Bibbs and Shady as family." She glanced down at her clasped hands hoping he was buying her explanation. The love part just popped out of her mouth, and she wished she could take it back.

Colt nodded. "I'm going to call the sheriff's office. Diane is right, he's gone too far."

Without him beside her, a coldness shrouded her. What did Billy want? If he wanted to talk, he could come to the front door instead of stalking her. Shivering, she wrapped her arms around her middle. Why wouldn't he just let her go? He must be mad she left him but to travel all this way from Texas was crazy.

"Shady and Bibbs just got back. They are heading to the house now. The sheriff will drop by when he can, talk about an arrogant piece of garbage." He walked to the door, opened it and nodded to his two cowhands.

"I think he drives a silver sedan," Shady said as he took off his hat. "I noticed it parked near the south watering hole. I was just about to ride toward it when I spotted a cow stuck in mud with her calf bawling next to her. I got her to safety and boy, was her calf happy. When I went back to where the car was parked it was gone."

"Does he have a silver car?" Colt asked as all three men turned and stared at Spring.

"We couldn't afford a car. My tips barely covered the rent, and he only worked sporadically. He thought he was too good to work at a restaurant or store despite that he never did graduate from high school and refused to get his GED. Choices he made led to unemployment, and I think he liked it that way. Maybe he stole the car."

"And you're positive it was him?" Colt handed her a cup of tea. "Decaf, you're already too wound up."

Bibbs picked up the switchblade Colt had tossed onto the table. "Haven't seen this baby since the time Caleb…" He trailed off and put it back down.

"I found it in a drawer in the kitchen. I wasn't about to let Billy hurt me again. I still think I should leave. I don't want any of you in danger from that lunatic."

Colt and Bibbs frowned at her while Shady sat on the couch next to her. "You're not going anywhere. We'll protect you. Besides, I like having you here. You make great cookies and all."

"Cookies?" Bibbs shook his head. "We think of you as part of our little family here and family takes care of its own. Come to think of it though, you do make darn good cookies."

Colt chuckled. "Do it for the cookies."

Spring nodded with a chuckle of her own. "Cookies are nice."

"In all seriousness we need to set up a plan to keep you safe. I think for now we'll go back to having one of us watching you at all times. Do you know how to shoot?"

Her eyes widened at Colt's question. "A gun?"

"Yes, a gun."

"None of the foster homes I stayed at let us touch guns."

Giving her a wink, he walked to the paneled wall on the left side of the fireplace and tapped on it. The panel popped open revealing his gun safe and he took out a small pistol. "This is a nine millimeter handgun. I think this one would be best for you to have."

"Me? How many guns do you have?"

"Enough. We'll start you off on the handgun then on to the rifle. I want you to be able to protect yourself."

The serious expression on his face brought the danger forefront. "I don't like guns, but you're right, I do need to be able to protect myself. Where's the shooting range?"

Bibbs and Shady exchanged amused grins.

"What's so funny?"

Colt put the gun back into the safe. "We have our own gun range here on the ranch."

"Let me guess. You have old cans and bottles set up to shoot at." Her body tingled as Colt wrapped his arm around her waist and pulled her to his side.

"Honey, we are not hicks. We have a fenced area with hay

bales we shoot at. Depending on the day we have a few different pictures we put on the bales to shoot at."

"What pictures?"

Colt grinned. "You'll see. Look who's driving up."

Following his gaze, she saw the police car finally drive up to the house. "Oh, great. Now he shows up, after the cavalry arrived."

Shady smiled and elbowed Bibbs. "Did you hear that? We're the cavalry."

"Buddy, you've been watching too many westerns," Bibbs replied, shaking his head. He walked to the door and opened it before Sheriff Brown had a chance to knock.

Without as much as a 'hello', the sheriff strode in and immediately stared at Colt's arm around Spring's waist. He smirked. "I knew you two had something going on."

Colt stiffened. "So what if we do? That's not why we called you. I guess there must have been a big delay in getting the message that you were needed."

The sheriff's eyes narrowed. "I don't like the tone of your voice. My schedule is my business. Besides I don't take much stock in what she has to say." He pointed at her accusingly.

Spring gasped. "Billy was here and—"

"And so what? I didn't get any reports of injuries." He looked her up and down, shrugged and stared her in the eye.

Colt stepped forward. "Don't make me call the state police again."

Sheriff Brown laughed. "Like it worked for you last time? Hell, you almost got arrested for horse stealing. Go ahead and call."

Spring stepped forward until she was shoulder to shoulder with Colt. Watching him run his fingers through his dark hair, she knew he shared her frustration. "Don't you have to write a report or something? Don't you need details?"

He crossed his arms in front of him. "Indeed I do need to

write a report, but I don't need details since I don't believe you. No one has seen this Billy character. I ran his name, he's not wanted."

Her eyes widened, and she blinked hard. "He's got a record!"

"Well, juvenile records can be sealed and his are."

"How convenient." It was so unbelievable, and she shook her head at the absurdity of it.

"Well, I have other business to take care of. Mrs. Grandy and Mrs. Ruth are fighting about the chickens." He turned and walked out the door.

Her shoulders slumped. "Who is fighting about chickens?"

"Those two old biddies drive everyone insane," Shady said. "Mrs. Grandy has a horse named Jasper, and whenever she needs Holden's help she pays him in chickens. Well Holden has no place for chickens so he gives them to Mrs. Ruth to keep. Well, Mrs. Ruth has a dog named Penny and she gives the chickens back when she needs the vet. So, Holden gives them back to Mrs. Grandy to hold onto."

With furrowed brow, she turned toward Colt. "Really?"

Colt nodded. "Been going on for a long time." His lips twitched.

"But by all rights, they really belong to Holden. So, what's the problem?"

"Holden wouldn't take payment from either of them, so the chicken exchange happens so the ladies don't get their feathers ruffled."

Bibbs laughed. "We wouldn't want any ruffled feathers. That was a good one, Boss."

Colt started to chuckle and immediately stopped. "In all seriousness, we have a big problem. I'll stay as close to Spring as I can, and you two can take turns watching her. I'm going to call my cousin Diane and let her know what that poor excuse of a sheriff said and tell her about the car Shady saw.

Bibbs, I'd appreciate it if you'd get Railroad taken care of. She is still in the corral."

"Not a problem. We'll get right on it." Bibbs put his hat on and slapped Shady on the shoulder. "Best get to it."

Shady nodded, grabbed his hat, and they walked out the door.

CHAPTER THIRTEEN

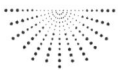

"$\mathscr{T}$he gun range is exactly how you described it." Spring watched as Colt explained gun safety. "Are those pictures of Sheriff Brown on those bales?"

Colt grinned. "They sure are. We also have pictures of Jacob Ash. He's a local that abuses horses. He buys them cheap, and sells them across the border. I use his picture a lot."

"This might be fun after all." Her smile lit up her whole face. How did she ever believe she wasn't pretty?

"What? Do I have something on my face?"

"Actually I was admiring your smile." He warmed as her face turned a deep shade of red. "Let's get started."

Leading her to the spot where the target was a bit closer, he felt her stiffen. "Relax." He handed her ear protectors, and she immediately put them on. Then he stood behind her with his arms around her, helping to aim the gun. She stiffened even more.

"I don't know if this is a good idea," she shouted

"Just take a deep breath and slowly let it out," he yelled back. He waited until she did it and relaxed somewhat. "Ease your finger on the trigger, nice and slow. Now pull back on the trigger."

She fired and started to turn around. He grabbed her and stopped her from moving. "Safety first. By the way, your hearing protector looks right sexy on you. Let's do it again."

They kept at it until her arms began to shake from the exertion of holding them in place for so long. He finally took the gun from her, and she walked out of the circle of his arms. He didn't need to guide her after the first few rounds but he'd enjoyed holding her.

"How'd I do?"

"A few more lessons and you'll be up there with the best. Then of course we do rifle training."

"You have the biggest shit eatin' grin on your face."

Colt secured the gun then turned toward her. He was in front of her in two long strides and gazing into her blue eyes. His happiness was in those eyes, a happiness he needed, a happiness he wanted. Swooping down, he claimed his happiness with a kiss. Her lips parted instantly, and her sweet noises sent him spiraling. He thought about making love to her right there on the grass but dismissed it as too public. The truck? No, their first time should be in a bed. His body responded to hers powerfully, and for a second, he regretted his choice to go shooting.

"Unless you want me to lay you down in the grass, we'd better stop."

She let go of him as he stepped away. Taking a deep breath, she nodded. "Yes of course, we need to stop." The desire in her eyes proved she felt differently, but he was on top of the world.

Taking her hand, he kissed her palm. "Life is short, we have no assurances of how long we will be here on earth. I'm just going to say this, and if you don't want to hear it, we can pretend I never said anything. I don't know how it happened;

I mean when you got here I swore never to care about you or anyone else again. I tried and tried to tell myself it was a bad idea, but it happened anyway. Spring, I love you." He averted his gaze not wanting to see an expression of doubt or disgust.

The silence stretched on until he finally turned and walked toward the truck.

"Wait! Don't you dare leave me. Colt, look at me!"

For a brief moment, he hesitated as his heart dropped but his need to know won out. As soon as he saw her face, he froze. Staring back at him, her eyes shone with her love, and he sighed in relief. "You're not upset?"

The sweetest smile crossed her face. "No, I'm not upset. I've been trying to squash my feelings for you. I grew up expecting the worst, with my back to the wall, watching life go by. Somehow, you changed me. I learned to trust, and hope, and to participate in my life. Colt, I love you too."

She walked into his open arms and put her arms around his neck. He gladly allowed her to pull him down for a kiss, a long passionate kiss filled with promises for their future. Now that their love was known, the kiss was even sweeter than before.

His cellphone rang, and he was so tempted to let it go to voicemail, but he had Bibbs and Shady out on the range, and he was responsible for them. The moment she stepped away, he longed to grab her back to him.

He glanced at the caller ID, and it was Bibbs. Frowning, he answered it.

"Boss, we have a situation here. You might want to take the package and go by way of the eagle."

"Bibbs? What are you talking about?"

"Amscray ithway ingspray."

"Is that Pig Latin? Bibbs, what's wrong with you?"

Shady must have grabbed Bibbs' phone. "Damn it, Bibbs,

listen, Boss, Peggy Jo is dead, and Ole Brownie is here to arrest our girl. Make tracks while you can."

"Stay there, and keep an eye on him. We'll be there as soon as we can."

"Are you sure you don't need to visit an old friend up in Canada or Mexico?" Shady asked.

"That's it, no more old westerns for you two. I'll get there when I can. Bye." Colt shook his head. They meant well, and any other time he'd laugh, but Spring was waiting for him to explain the call.

"Honey, your…I mean Peggy Jo is dead, and the sheriff is waiting to arrest you."

Immediately, she covered her mouth, as her eyes grew wide. Shaking her head, she dropped her hand again. "How the heck did Peggy Jo get herself killed?"

"They didn't say."

"They?"

"Bibbs was talking in Pig Latin, and Shady was telling us to cross the border, any border. The sheriff is at the house." He shifted his weight from one leg to another. "I don't think making a run for it is the answer."

Her face turned pale. "I don't like this, Colt. He's been gunning for me."

"I'll call Diane and have her meet us at the house. We could shoot a few more rounds at the sheriff's face." He pulled her into his arms, kissed her cheek then let her go. "Diane might even enjoy tangling with the sheriff."

SPRING'S MIND whirled the whole way back to the house. Why would the sheriff think she'd done it? He must be out of his mind! Of course, with the constant watch on her, she had an alibi but something else must be going on. "I thought I'd feel more. I mean I spent my whole life wishing she'd come and rescue me and in the end, I just wanted her gone. Guess I shouldn't say the gone part to the police. Do you think Billy had something to do with her death? I don't think they knew each other but they have been around. Maybe they ran into each other?"

Her heartbeat sped up but as soon as Colt took her hand in his comforting one, she calmed a bit.

"They have no proof, honey. We'll have Diane take care of it."

Normally she enjoyed the view as they drove but now it was all a blur going by. *Damn it, Peggy Jo. Why'd you get yourself killed when I finally found happiness?* She glanced at Colt's profile. He loved her. What had been the best day of her life was now a disaster. "I wouldn't blame you if you walked away from me."

Colt slowed the truck and pulled off onto the side of the road. He unbuckled both of their seat belts and pulled her close. "That's not how love works. I love you, and I believe in you. I'll be by your side every step of the way."

Tears rolled slowly down her face. "No one ever believed in me before."

"Caleb did, and he sent you to me. I know it must be scary and upsetting, but I've got your back." He held her and stroked her back until she felt composed.

"Thank you. Let's go and see what the sheriff has to say."

Colt smiled at her. "Chin up."

"Yes, chin up." Colt was right. Caleb had believed in her.

When she saw Diane's car was parked next to the police car, Spring's fear eased. Colt parked the car and opened her door for her. "You've got this."

Taking his hand, she nodded. "With you beside me, I've got this."

The front door swung open and Sheriff Brown, Diane,

Shady and Bibbs all spilled out. Both Shady and Bibbs looked afraid while Diane and the sheriff both sported determined expressions. In fact, Sheriff Brown's face was a startling shade of red.

"'Bout time you showed up." The sheriff's voice sounded a bit menacing. "Spring Reed, I have a warrant for your arrest."

Colt stepped forward. "What are the charges?" His ability to remain cool was admirable.

"Murder. Her ma is at the county morgue. I can't say I'm surprised."

Swallowing hard, Spring shook her head. "You're wrong." She glanced at Diane. "I assume I should keep my mouth shut until I'm questioned."

"Yes, don't say a word until I'm in the room with you. Go peacefully with Brownie. I'll be right behind you."

Spring gave Shady and Bibbs a weak smile then she turned to Colt. They locked gazes the whole time she was being handcuffed. "I'll see you soon?"

"Count on it and remember, you've got this."

She lifted her chin in response and walked to the police car. It was hard to believe this was her second ride in handcuffs inside of a week.

"I've got you this time. I even have a witness. There won't be a thing that sneaky lawyer of yours can do to help you. To think I thought it was a run of the mill type of day. It's turning out to be the best day I've had in a long time."

He watched her in the rearview mirror, and she bit the inside of her cheek to keep from responding. She hoped she appeared aloof because she felt anything but. Thinking about Colt, helped. He loved her, even if it was hard to embrace the whole concept right away. He did mean it when he said he had her back, didn't he?

Old habits and learned responses were hard to break. One by one, Colt had broken through her barriers all except for one: doubt. If he didn't mean all the things he said today, she'd never get over it.

"Something wrong back there?"

"What? No, I'm fine." She must have given away her feelings.

He parked the car and grabbed her out of it. They went through the door, and her heart jumped at the scene. Stone, Jonas and Holden were surrounding an angry Billy.

"What are you fools doing here?" The sheriff demanded. "Unhand my witness."

"The lug is your witness?" Holden stared at the sheriff in disbelief. "Mindy Sue called and told us Billy was here."

"Why are you here? Get lost all of you."

"No can do," Jonas responded.

"The state police are on their way, and they asked us to keep this lug in custody," Stone explained.

"Something about a stolen car?" Holden shrugged.

"Are you going to uncuff me?" Spring asked. This farce was obviously crumbling to pieces.

"No, missy I am not. I'm putting you in a cell where you belong." He pulled her past everyone and shoved her in cell. It was located at the back of the building and it was so quiet, too quiet.

"How'd Peggy Jo die?" she asked.

The cell door closed, echoing through the corridor. "Overdose." He smirked. "And Billy is willing to testify you bought the heroin that killed her. You know you shouldn't have hired Diane as your lawyer. Never did like her, and there is no way she is going to win this game." He cackled as he left.

Sitting on the bunk, she wondered what the heck was going on. A 'game'? Peggy Jo was dead, she was in jail and Billy was walking? Free for now, anyway. People didn't take kindly to having their cars stolen.

Her heart sank. Peggy Jo was dead, and she didn't expect to feel anything but it was all beginning to sink in. Her mother overdosed. Spring's eyes filled but she refused to let the tears fall. Peggy Jo didn't deserve tears. *Damn you! Why couldn't you have been like other mothers?* A few tears escaped and trailed down her face. They were tears of a child who wanted her mother. She was no longer a child so she quickly wiped her tears away.

Diane would sort it out, and she'd be free in no time. She sighed deeply. The sheriff seemed more than determined to convict her. It was her biggest frustration in life, being used as a pawn with no control over the outcome. She'd honestly thought she could put her past behind her and start a new life.

Shaking her head, she marveled at her naivety. She'd brought danger to Colt's door in her quest to be free. He probably was rethinking everything about her. What if he didn't love her anymore? Her heart beat painfully against her ribs. Leaning against the cool brick wall, she closed her eyes and relived their kiss and his declaration of love.

Her eyes flew open, and her mouth dropped. She was a fool to doubt him; he was as true blue as they came. Her doubts came from within, and a lot of them had to do with that piece of trash Billy. That jerk still had a hold on her.

Getting to her feet, she paced in the tiny cell. Slowly she walked, the last of her barriers melted away, leaving her heart full. What a difference it made, getting Billy out of her head. There was a sense of serenity she'd never known before. It wouldn't have been possible to get to this point without Colt.

Footsteps filled the hall, and she expected to see the sheriff. To her delight, it was Colt walking a brisk path to her cell.

"What are you doing back here? Is this a jailbreak?" She

gave him a cocky smile, much like the one he always gave her.

"It looks like this cell and the one right next to it are going to be needed."

"Really?"

Colt unlocked the door and unlocked her handcuffs. "I can't believe he left these on you."

"What's going on?"

"Billy is going to take your place. It appears he likes to steal cars, deal drugs, assault women and murder."

"Really?"

"I'll explain more later." He took her hand. "Let's get you out of here."

"Wait, who is the other cell for?"

"Sheriff—or I should say ex-Sheriff Brown will be in the other cell. The state police have been watching him for a while, thanks to Diane. When they arrived a minute ago, they made the double-arrest."

Her head wanted to explode with all the information. "Let's go!"

All she wanted to do was head home with her cowboy, but before she could go, she had to sit and give the state police her statement. It felt like an eternity of sitting in a chair, recounting her trials. Apparently, she wasn't the first person Sheriff Brown tried to railroad. He believed himself to be judge and jury. Officer Tonas of the State Police mentioned something about an old high school grudge the sheriff had against Summer, Jonas, Colt and a few others.

"I grew up here and old Brownie wasn't well liked. He was a bully then and he used his position as an officer of the peace to keep bullying."

"I'd like to see Billy if it's all right? I have a few things I need to say to him."

Officer Tonas lifted his brow and gave her a puzzled look. "Are you sure you want to see him?"

"I need to do this."

He stood and escorted her to the back, leading her to Billy's cell. "I'll be right outside the door, knock when you're ready to leave.

Spring nodded, and then gave Billy her full attention. He didn't look so cock sure of himself behind steel bars. He stared at her with cold, angry eyes that would have frightened her in the past.

"What are you doing here? You know you're just like every other female I've ever known—good for nothing." His voice sounded menacing but she didn't care.

"I thought you were my protector, but I now see, you were my tormentor. Strong men don't beat women and they sure don't kill them. You had me fooled for a long time, Billy, but my eyes are wide open and I know better. I'm just glad I left when I did."

"Well, you were just my whore. You didn't mean a thing to me. Now I suppose you're O'Malley's whore."

If he were waiting for her to flinch, he'd be disappointed. "I was never a whore, Billy, you just made me think I was. You know what? I'm not good for nothing, in fact I have great value in the work I do. I'm not the ugly girl you made me believe I was. I'm glad to be rid of you and your hatred of the world." She watched as his nostrils flared and the veins in his neck became visible.

"If I could I'd kill you," he sneered.

"I know you would. Good bye Billy."

She walked to the door and knocked. Billy swore to get her back and kill her and as soon as Officer Tonas opened the door, she rushed through it. A feeling of strength and triumph ran through her and she sighed in relief.

Eagerly she made her way toward the door and gave Diane, Holden, Stone and Jonas all hugs.

She walked to the truck hand in hand with her handsome cowboy and smiled as he helped her in. As soon as she got into Colt's truck, she slumped back against the seat.

"Tired?"

Reaching out, she caressed his strong jaw. "I can't believe so much happened in one day. I love you, Colt. I believe in you too."

He swooped in for a breathtaking kiss. "Hope you catch your second wind when we get home."

Her cheeks burned but her heart sang.

IT WASN'T her first time but her nerves got to her while she waited in Colt's bed still dressed. They were kissing, and he announced he forgot to do something. He hadn't left the house; she didn't hear the door open or close.

What if—No, no more doubts. He loved her and that was that.

She smiled when he came back into the room holding a small box.

"I bought this a week ago in hope. Well, here goes." He sat on the bed facing her. "Spring Reed, will you do me the honor of being my wife?" Opening the box, he revealed a gold, sparkly, pear shaped, diamond engagement ring.

Surprised, she stared at him then looked at the ring. She gasped, "It's so beautiful you don't have the money for this ring."

He frowned. "This was one of the cheaper ones. I figured I could buy you a bigger one sometime down the road."

She nodded and he looked confused. "Yes! I will marry you."

Colt put the diamond ring on her finger and smiled. "I was hoping you'd say yes."

"Kiss me, cowboy."

Colt leaned in for a kiss, a deep passionate kiss. Soon he had her flat on her back as he kissed her neck. "We need less clothes on," he said, his voice husky.

"That's easy enough to take care of." She pulled off her T-shirt and unhooked her navy blue bra. "Hey, quit staring and get undressed." She laughed as she teased him.

"Happy to oblige ma'am."

She took the opportunity to watch as he took off his shirt, drooling at his hard chest and chiseled abs. When he lowered his pants and finally his underwear, she gasped. "I—will it fit?"

Colt frowned. "You and Billy were together, weren't you?"

"Yes, but it was… well. Never mind. Forget it. Let's not ruin the moment." She shimmied out of the rest of her clothes and was rewarded with an appreciative look.

"You are so damn sexy." Colt laid her on her back and started at her toes, kissing his way up her thighs. He stopped at the juncture of her thighs, making her squirm with his mouth.

"Oh, I didn't know…"

Colt glanced at her face. "Really? He sounds like a selfish bastard. Don't you worry I'll make your body hum."

She raised her right eyebrow. "Oh, yeah?"

Instead of answering, he continued his assault with his tongue until she cried out in pleasure. Wave after wave of a feeling so intense she had no words for it.

Kissing the insides of her thighs again, he gazed at her with his cocky grin. Slowly he moved from her thighs, to her navel, and he played homage to her breasts. He suckled one nipple then the other, and the need to have him inside her was all-consuming. It seemed to take him forever to make his way up to her neck.

Shivering she ran her hands through his hair, guiding his sensual lips to hers. She opened her mouth to deepen the kiss. Kissing him was pure joy, and her body hummed.

She opened her legs at his prompting, and he entered her in one stroke.

Her eyes widened in surprise. He filled her beyond capacity and she loved it. When he pulled all the way out, she felt bereft but then he plunged into her again and again until she couldn't think. Her nails dug into his back but he didn't seem to notice. He went on and on until she cried out again, and then he threw his head back groaning. Shuddering, he moved within her a few more times and just before he swooped down for another kiss, she saw his love shining in his eyes. His lips were so tender as was the kiss and it filled her heart.

"I love you," he whispered against her lips.

Stunned and basking in the aftermath of pleasure, she was speechless. Instead, she grabbed him around the neck and kissed him with every ounce of love she had, laughing as he turned them over until he was on his back. He lifted her until she was astride him. "Again?" she asked.

"Hold on tight, honey. You're in for a long ride."

EPILOGUE

 *year later...*

SPRING DROVE HOME QUICKLY. She couldn't wait to talk to Colt, and she knew he'd be as excited as she was. They'd been married just about eight months now, and it had finally happened. Her heart filled knowing she was giving her husband the one thing he craved, a family.

They were so happy together but he still had his bouts of missing Caleb. She didn't think the pain ever went away. Some didn't recover from a loss like that.

Colt stood in the drive waiting for her when she pulled up. He hurried and opened the car door for her. "Pop the trunk, and I'll get the packages."

Standing, she smiled. "There aren't any packages, Colt. Well at least not in the trunk."

Colt frowned as he stared at her. "You didn't buy anything?"

"No. I have a much better present for you."

"Aw, honey, you didn't have to get me anything."

Laughing, she wrapped her arms around his waist. "We are going to have a package delivered in about eight months."

The look of awareness spreading across his face was priceless. He gave her a sexy, smile. "Are you sure?"

"Yes, I was just at the doctor's office. It's official, we're pregnant!"

Pulling her closer, he buried his face in her hair then he pulled back enough to see her face. "You are so amazing."

Her face heated. "I had some help you know."

"Good, fun, wholesome help. Is it a boy? Oh, wow another cowboy. What should we name him?"

"Why do men automatically assume it will be a boy? A girl would be just as nice."

Colt kissed her lips then swung her up into his brawny arms. "A girl would be just as nice. Truthfully, I feel so blessed right now. Let's get you inside and lying down." He carried her across the drive, up the porch steps and into the house. "Bed or couch?"

Shaking her head, she laughed. "On my feet would be best. I don't have to lie down. I'm perfectly healthy."

He set her on the couch and sat next to her. "We'll make a schedule. I'll watch you most of the time, and Shady and Bibbs can help. We've done it before we can do it again."

"Colt, be serious."

"Do you want me to hire some live-in help?"

God love him, the concern on his face was endearing, but if she didn't set him straight right from the start, she'd have to wrestle control from him. "You know I love you right?"

"Of course and I love you too."

"When you watched me before, I was in danger. Billy is serving life in prison without possibility of parole.

"I'm glad the lug admitted to killing that girl for stealing your ring. For someone who acted so tough, he sure did crumble under questioning. Tonas said, as soon as Billy opened his mouth he couldn't seem to stop incriminating himself. "

"So, we can agree the danger is gone, right?"

"What are you getting at?"

"I know you mean well but if you guys watch me I swear I'll hit you all up the side of your heads with an iron skillet."

Colt stared at her in surprise and then started to laugh. "Too overbearing? I just want to take care of you."

Leaning over, she gave him a deep loving kiss before sitting herself on his lap. She began to squirm against him as she kissed him.

"I know what you're doing."

"And what would that be, my big, handsome cowboy?"

"You're trying to distract me."

"Well, is it working?" She stared into his passion-filled chocolate eyes.

"What do you think?" He stroked her cheek tenderly.

"I hope it's working. I want to celebrate." She batted her eyelashes at him.

"Is it safe with the baby and all?"

"I'm going to the bookstore tomorrow. There must be a book for clueless fathers to be."

"I'm a genius in the bedroom." He winked at her.

"Come on, cowboy, and show me that intellectual side."

Spring laughed as Colt stood with her in his arms.

"Bedroom?" Colt asked.

"You know it cowboy. By the way, I love you."

Colt stopped and smiled at her. "I love you too."

ABOUT THE AUTHOR

Sexy Cowboys and the Women Who Love Them...
Finalist in the 2012 and 2015 RONE Awards.
Top Pick, Five Star Series from the Romance Review.
Kathleen Ball writes contemporary and historical western
romance with great emotion and
memorable characters. Her books are award winners and
have appeared on best sellers lists including: Amazon's Best
Seller's List, All Romance Ebooks, Bookstrand, Desert
Breeze Publishing and Secret Cravings Publishing Best
Sellers list. She is the recipient of eight Editor's Choice
Awards, and The Readers' Choice Award for Ryelee's
Cowboy.
Winner of the Lear diamond award Best Historical Novel-
Cinders' Bride
There's something about a cowboy

facebook.com/kathleenballwesternromance
twitter.com/kballauthor
instagram.com/author_kathleenball

So Many Roads to Choose

The Settlers

Greg

Juan

Scarlett

Mail Order Brides of Spring Water

Tattered Hearts

Shattered Trust

Glory's Groom

Battered Soul

Romance on the Oregon Trail

Cora's Courage

Luella's Longing

Dawn's Destiny

Terra's Trial

Candle Glow and Mistletoe

The Kabvanagh Brothers

Teagan: Cowboy Strong

Quinn: Cowboy Risk

Brogan: Cowboy Pride

Sullivan: Cowboy Protector

Donnell: Cowboy Scrutiny

Murphy: Cowboy Deceived

Fitzpatrick: Cowboy Reluctant

Angus: Cowboy Bewildered

Rafferty: Cowboy Trail Boss

Shea: Cowboy Chance

Made in the USA
Monee, IL
24 March 2022